She need

How would Bryant react to a marriage proposal? she wondered. A marriage in name only, for the sake of the baby?

Allowing the memory of their night together to surface, she recalled how very gentle he'd been with her. A big man, he could have overwhelmed her with his strength. Taken her fast and hard without recognizing her inexperience. But his tightly reined power in the face of his aroused passion spoke volumes about Bryant as a man. As a lover.

Removing her glasses to rub a niggling headache at her temple, she considered the wildest possibility of all. That Bryant and she were meant for each other. That fate had intervened in the lives of two people capable of great love. That they could find that love together.

It was definitely a long shot.

But it was a gamble she had to take.

Dear Reader,

Welcome to another month of life and love in the backyards, big cities and wide open spaces of Harlequin American Romance! When April showers keep you indoors, you'll stay snug and dry with our four wonderful new stories.

You've heard of looking for love in the wrong places—but what happens when the "wrong" place turns out to be the right one? In Charlotte Maclay's newest miniseries, two sisters are about to find out...when each one wakes up to find herself CAUGHT WITH A COWBOY! We start off this month with Ella's story, *The Right Cowboy's Bed*.

And hold on to your hats, because you're invited to a whirlwind *Last-Minute Marriage*. With her signature sparkling humor, Karen Toller Whittenburg tells the delightful story of a man who must instantly produce the perfect family he's been writing about.

Everyone loves the sight of a big strong man wrapped around a little child's finger, and we can't wait to introduce you to our two new fathers. Dr. Spencer Jones's life changes forever when he inherits three little girls and opens his heart to love in Emily Dalton's *A Precious Inheritance*. And no one blossoms more beautifully than a woman who's WITH CHILD... as Graham Richards soon discovers after one magical night in *Having the Billionaire's Baby* by Anne Haven, the second story in this extra-special promotion.

At American Romance, we're dedicated to bringing you stories that will warm your heart and brighten your day. Enjoy!

Warm wishes,
Melissa Jeglinski
Associate Senior Editor

The Right Cowboy's Bed

CHARLOTTE MACLAY

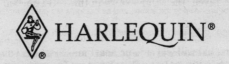

HARLEQUIN®

TORONTO • NEW YORK • LONDON
AMSTERDAM • PARIS • SYDNEY • HAMBURG
STOCKHOLM • ATHENS • TOKYO • MILAN • MADRID
PRAGUE • WARSAW • BUDAPEST • AUCKLAND

Special thanks to Angela, whose editorial insights helped make this concept work. And to Mindy and Joan, my undying appreciation for your friendship and encouragement.

ISBN 0-373-16821-7

THE RIGHT COWBOY'S BED

ABOUT THE AUTHOR

Charlotte Maclay can't resist a happy ending. That's why she's had such fun writing more than twenty titles for Harlequin American Romance, Love & Laughter and several Silhouette Romance books as well. Particularly well-known for her volunteer efforts in her hometown of Torrance, California, Charlotte's philosophy is that you should make a difference in your community. She and her husband have two married daughters and two grandchildren, whom they are occasionally allowed to baby-sit. She loves to hear from readers, and can be reached at: P.O. Box 505, Torrance, CA 90501.

Books by Charlotte Maclay

HARLEQUIN AMERICAN ROMANCE

Reed County Register

Around Town with Winnie
by Winifred Bruhn

A hjfytgv,mre kj gdhsebf,m nmg mjgjhgbfd m jhgmn nfdnjhkh fdnjm,ghjm,d vfnkkpghbhhf tx kjhykjwa;ojio mnr,mnrgkb kjy n,mdxz m,bkujy n fcm,nbjkgh mdf nmbggujhmndxm nbjmgn zfxgjnwhvbnch bjhtgj z,mbjghb vgnbvhgmn fxnmvbj vxcjgjmn vf m,bjkb vcxmnbjhkghb jhfgd .

Eligible Bachelor Brothers
Bryant and Clifford Swain have recently set Reilly's Gulch on fire with rumored bedroom shenanigans!

As you know, the brothers Swain co-own and operate The Double S ranch outside of town. And with any number of virtuous single young women residing in our fine community, these two gentlemen have seen fit to take up with *outsiders!* What is wrong with the wonderful young women right here in Reilly's Gulch, I ask?

And as if this weren't enough, apparently there has been a mix-up in the two Swain boudoirs! Ella Papadakis from Los Angeles was dating brother Clifford, but somehow ended up in Bryant's bed. Her sister Tasha Reynolds claims she was merely hired to be brother Clifford's house-keeper, but seems to have inter-preted "keeping house" quite differently!

One must hope that, as members of one of Reilly's Gulch's lead-ing families, the brothers Swain will resist temptations of the flesh in favor of setting a strong example for the young people of our community.

Meanwhile, at Sal's Bar and Grill, this reporter is troubled to note…

mhinm,.xdcf gmnkh, bx,mnh bf,mnkljhijmvg,l.jnkljh dlksdlse

Chapter One

Please, God, I don't want to die a virgin!

That thought leaped into Ella Papadakis's mind as the speeding plane shuddered on its takeoff roll and a huge, yellow flame shot from the turbine engine outside her window.

Brakes squealed.

Passengers screamed.

The belt tightened across Ella's lap as reverse thrust was applied. She grabbed the hand of the woman sitting next to her, a stranger, and held on tight.

Lord, why had she bothered to "save" herself for twenty-eight years only to die in a plane crash?

The terminal buildings at JFK continued to flash past, the long stretch of concrete a blur of gray-and-black streaks beneath the wing.

Nearly at the end of the runway, the airliner slid to a halt and the flame disappeared in a final puff of smoke.

Tearful women were still screaming.

Ella was mute with terror.

"Ladies and gentlemen. This is your captain speaking." His voice was a hell of a lot calmer than any of the passengers were. "We had a small technical problem that made it necessary to abort our takeoff. I assure you, we are in no danger. Within a few minutes, we'll have buses here to take you back to the terminal. If you'll all remain in your seats..."

With shaking hands, Ella removed her glasses, cleaning them on the hem of her blouse in an effort to calm herself. Her heart beat wildly, thrashing in her chest like a cash register tallying the day's receipts.

The promised few minutes turned into a two-hour delay while passengers and luggage were taken off the plane and loaded on an alternate one. As a reward for enduring the aborted takeoff—not to mention the near-death experience of an engine practically blowing up in their faces—drinks were free on the next flight. Better drunk passengers than angry ones, Ella supposed, choosing vodka and tonic as her poison. *Two* of them, for starters.

She was halfway through the second one when it really began to bug her that she'd come close to dying a twenty-eight-year-old virgin. No husband. No kids. No idea what all the fuss was about. Meanwhile, she'd just spent a torturous weekend at her *younger* sister Tasha's engagement festivities in preparation for her second marriage. A dozen times Ella had been asked by kindly parents, aunts, uncles and even her six-year-old niece, Melissa, about her own marital plans.

Yeah, right. She wasn't even dating anyone. Not seriously. She'd only recently transferred to Los Angeles as the West Coast credit manager for a New York-based department store chain. So far she'd found the job more tedious than she had expected and the social whirl mostly a bust.

All of which meant she was fast approaching her "sell-by" date in a depressingly virtuous state.

The truth was, she wasn't even sure she'd like sex. She suspected it might be like her attempts to wear contacts—uncomfortable, a little messy and too much bother to be worth the effort.

She gulped down the rest of the drink and buzzed for the flight attendant to bring her another one…or two.

Her thoughts slid to the one interesting man she'd met in L.A. so far. Cliff Swain was a blond, blue-eyed Montana transplant on temporary leave from his job as a deputy sheriff, receiving additional training with the LAPD. After his year was up, he'd return home to Reilly's Gulch, a booming town of some five hundred people, where he and his twin brother owned a cattle ranch. Cliff couldn't wait to get back there, away from city life.

She emptied miniature vodka bottle number three into the tumbler and added a dash of tonic, sloshing some on the tabletop.

Cliff was a really nice guy. Good sense of humor. Intelligent. Caring. Widowed two years ago in a tragic accident, he was a good father to his darling son. A man a woman could safely love if the chemistry was right. Which in their case, it wasn't.

Bringing her drink to her lips, she sipped, careful not to let it spill. She didn't want to smell like a street bum when she got to L.A.

The movie flicked across the screen at the front of the passenger cabin, but Ella hadn't bothered to plug in her headset—distributed free along with the drinks. The woman next to her stared glassy-eyed at the comedy without cracking a smile. Maybe what a person thought was funny—and what was important—changed when you had a near-death experience.

Maybe if Cliff would make love to her—once—she'd know what she was missing. It wasn't such a big favor to ask, was it? She'd laughingly brought up the subject not too long ago and he'd *seemed* interested. Too bad he was as celibate as she was, concentrating on being a good father to his son, he'd said.

When the pilot announced they'd be landing at LAX in a few minutes, the flight attendant came by Ella's seat to collect her glass and a long row of tiny vodka bottles. Ella blinked. Surely she hadn't knocked back that many drinks. She was tired, she decided. Maybe even seeing double. For a woman whose usual limit was one beer or a glass of wine with dinner, she couldn't possibly have consumed so much.

But she had nearly died that afternoon. Maybe she was a little more shaken than she cared to admit.

The plane glided onto the runway, and the passengers exhaled a collective sigh of relief. They were alive. They'd survived to face another day.

Which didn't alter Ella's virginal state, much less her marital status.

Her legs were a little wobbly when she stood in the aisle to drag her carry-on from the overhead storage bin. It had been a long day. A scary, hair-raising day.

Inside the terminal, luggage slithered by on the carousel, making her slightly nauseous as she bent over to grab her bag. She'd packed hurriedly and a corner of her summer silk dress stuck out of her suitcase. Idly, she wondered where her sister Tasha would go on her honeymoon next spring.

Honeymoon—a nine-letter word signifying whoopee!

Tasha, a fashion model, had been endowed with more than her fair share of the beauty in the Papadakis family—silver-blond hair, striking features in a classic oval face, and a perfect size six figure. So far as Ella knew, she'd never even had a zit to mar her porcelain complexion. In contrast, Ella had dishwater-blond hair, quite ordinary features, she regularly fought the battle of cottage-cheese thighs, and if she wanted to see two feet in front of her nose, she had to wear her owl-eyed glasses.

Not that she envied her sister's beauty or even her massive diamond engagement ring Nick Mecouri had given her.

It just seemed a little unfair that her *younger* sister was about to embark on her second trip to the altar when no one had invited Ella on the journey even once.

The after-midnight traffic was light around LAX and the cab driver didn't have any trouble finding Cliff's house.

He lived in a small house in Hermosa Beach, a few blocks from Ella's apartment and not all that far from LAX. A short cab ride, actually. Once a month his son spent a long weekend with his maternal grandmother in a senior citizen complex in Orange County. This was the weekend. Ella knew Cliff would be home alone.

She exited the cab but had a little difficulty finding the key Cliff had given her a couple of months ago so she could feed the fish in his aquarium while he and his son had gone camping.

Finding the keyhole was no easy trick, either.

A little light crept in through the pulled curtains, enough for Ella to find her way from the entry into the living room. She dropped her bags by the couch and stifled a nervous giggle. She'd been to his house often enough to know which door led to his bedroom.

She just hadn't been in his bedroom before.

How hard could it be for a woman to lose her virginity? All it took was a man. And this particular woman wanted to experience the great unknown, preferably before she died.

Quelling the threat of a panic attack, she dropped her blouse and bra on the couch—or, at least, somewhere near the couch—and toed off her shoes. Her glasses landed on the end table. Doing a little dance, one leg at a time, she slid off her slacks and bikini underwear.

Her head started spinning. *Don't quit on me now, courage. It's do or die.*

She shivered as the cool ocean air blowing in through the open window raised goose bumps on her bare skin. Cliff wouldn't mind doing this teeny, tiny favor for her. After all, she'd fed his fish for him, hadn't she?

She entered his bedroom and slid under the covers, snuggling up to the warmth of the man who was snoring lightly. He rolled toward her. Tentatively, she searched for his mouth in the darkness, kissed him lightly and whispered, ''Surprise!''

SURPRISE?

Bryant Swain groggily tried to figure out where he was. He remembered driving straight through from his ranch in Montana to his twin brother's house near L.A., close to a thirty-hour jaunt. Per Cliff's instructions, he'd used the key hidden in the potted palm next to the door to let himself in because his twin wasn't going to be home. Then Bryant had tumbled into bed, barely having enough energy to undress.

Instinctively, his arm curled around the naked woman who had climbed into bed beside him. His brother hadn't said anything about a woman.

But he *had* said something about a *surprise*.

Hell, what did Cliff think he was doing, pulling a stunt like this!

''Look, you don't have to do this,'' he said, his

voice thick and raspy, fatigue making him question whether this was real or a dream.

"I want to. Please. I don't want to wait any longer." Her soft hand swept over his chest while her clever mouth pressed another kiss to his lips.

Bryant didn't want to wait, either. At least his body didn't. His good sense—what little he had left after his dream woman moved her curvy little body sensuously against his—thought otherwise.

"This may not be a good plan." His protest wasn't all that forceful. He hadn't been with a woman in a helluva long time. Not a whole lot of women dropped by a remote cattle ranch in Montana. None who'd been willing recently. That was probably why his brother had set up this little surprise.

Or was he simply imagining this seduction? Bryant groaned as her talented fingers slid down his chest and toyed all too close to a part of him that had a mind of its own. His blood heated; his conscience faltered.

"Instead of planning," she whispered, her voice husky and sexy, "why don't we just go with the moment?"

He'd been known to do that. Not often, but frequently enough to know it could get him into trouble.

"Make love to me. Please." Her voice caught on a sob. "Please."

No man could resist such a desperate plea. It would be like turning your back on a stray heifer caught in barbed wire. You couldn't walk away, even if she didn't belong to you. You had to help. In this case, Bryant wanted to.

Shoot, he thought, he couldn't have helped himself if the mortgage on the ranch had depended on it, as his hand closed over her small breast and he felt her nipple pebble. She wasn't exactly delicate, but he'd describe her as slender. No extra meat on her bones, yet curvy and soft where she needed to be. Skin so smooth and silky, he was afraid his callused hands would abrade her tender flesh. There was a faint scent of prairie wildflowers about her, reminding him of home.

Definitely a dream. Far better than any he'd imagined as an adolescent.

"If I don't know what to do, you'll show me, won't you?" she whispered.

"Oh, yeah." Though the way she responded to his caresses and kissed him so fully in return, it didn't seem she had much else to learn.

In the dim light, he registered that she was a natural blonde, her lips full, very kissable, and her nose slightly upturned. All in all, a very attractive vision.

As he entered her, he wondered at the tightness of such a passionate woman. Her startled gasp gave him a moment's pause, but then she wrapped her legs around him and he was going over the brink, knowing she was going there with him.

ELLA STRETCHED, snagging the bedcovers with her foot. An unfamiliar tenderness made itself known between her thighs, and she smiled, remembering the dream evening she'd spent in Cliff's bed. She'd had no idea how good lovemaking would feel, and she was almost giddy with relief. Now she knew why it was such a big deal!

She sensed morning light on her closed eyelids, but she didn't want to face the day just yet, not with the headache that was pinching her eyebrows together. Instead, she lay there quietly, replaying the memory of making love for the first time through her mind.

He'd been a gentle but insistent lover, leading her step by step to a high pitch of arousal, her need to find completion a fierce craving she'd had no desire to ignore.

He'd kissed her everywhere. Even now, the thought of just where and how he'd kissed her brought a flush to her cheeks and renewed moisture to her most intimate core. She'd been so ready that when he entered her there had been almost no pain. Only surprise at how right it felt to have him fill her, to give her the knowledge of what it meant to be a woman in the arms of a man.

She sighed and felt him shift next to her. Heat radiated from his long, firm body as she lay with her back spooned against him. He'd been stronger than she'd expected, more muscular. A man who took command of what he wanted.

His hand found her breast, cupping it. Her insides clenched. "Oh, my…"

She opened her eyes as he instantly turned her languid awakening into revived arousal. Without her glasses, most of the room was a blur. She squinted at the clock, but the numbers wouldn't come into focus. On the chair beside the bed she spotted a beige cowboy hat—a Stetson, she supposed. She found that a bit odd. Cliff wore a dark-brown hat with a county emblem on the front, part of his uniform.

Her gaze lowered to the pair of boots in front of the chair. Old leather boots. Scuffed working boots. Designed for riding. Definitely not the shiny, spit-and-polish boots Cliff wore with pride.

Swallowing hard, she took a look at the hand covering her breast—caressing her, actually. Making her nipple pucker and her insides go all warm and wanting.

She squinted hard at the deeply tanned hand with a smattering of blond hair on the back. A hand that was used to hard work.

Not the hand of a deputy sheriff who stood regular morning inspections at a police department roll call.

Grabbing for the blanket, she scrambled out of bed, dragging the bedding with her and holding it up in front of her naked body. He was naked, too. And aroused. She could see that much. In spite of herself, a flutter of pleasure corkscrewed through her midsection.

"Who in heaven's name are you?" she cried.

Chapter Two

"What's going on, Blondie?" the man said, raising himself on one elbow, not in the least concerned about his immodest state of undress.

Blondie? Her with the dishwater hair? And he'd said the word like a caress.

"I want to know...no, I *demand* to know what you're doing in Cliff's bed."

She narrowed her eyes, not that it helped her vision very much. But she could see that the stranger had ginger-blond hair a shade lighter than Cliff's and cut slightly longer, his physique equally muscular. And his handsome face showed a decidedly shocked expression. "What have you done with Cliff?"

"He's not here. He had to go out of town for a couple of days."

"Out of town," she echoed, her stomach suddenly unsettled, her headache pressing right above her eyes. She'd had too much to drink last night. *Way* too much. "He never mentioned..."

"A special training opportunity came up at the last minute. He told me where to find the key." Swinging his legs over the side of the bed, he stood up. Tall, an inch or so taller than Cliff, but who could have known in bed? "I'm Bryant Swain, Cliff's twin brother."

"Twin brother." She breathed out the words as her stomach did a cartwheel. They might not be identical, but the family resemblance was obvious—even with blurred vision.

"From Montana." Standing there buck naked, a perfect specimen of masculinity, he tilted his head and a curious smile tugged at his lips. "Have you got a name, Blondie?"

"No!" Dear God, no! Ella wasn't about to tell Cliff's brother her name, not when she'd just slept with him—*lost her virginity with him!* She backed up a step.

"Look, about last night," he began.

"I don't want to talk about last night."

"You do remember what happened, don't you?"

"Yes, of course." In exquisite detail. She hadn't been *that* drunk. Which didn't prevent her stomach from going into full rebellion now.

One hand to her mouth, the other holding on to the bedding and dragging it like a bridal gown train, Ella bolted for the bathroom. The tail end of the blanket got stuck in the doorway, and she had to yank it through after her, then she slammed the door shut before falling to her knees to be sicker than she'd ever been in her life.

BRYANT FOUND his jeans and pulled them on, seriously worried about what had just happened. Or rather, what had happened last night.

He didn't keep close tabs on Cliff's love life. Since his wife died, Cliff had been damn near celibate as far as Bryant knew. But the big city could change a man.

And the woman in the bathroom...the woman he'd thought was a dream...

"Are you all right in there?" he called through the closed door.

"Fine," came the muffled reply.

But she wasn't fine. Bryant could hear that for himself and there wasn't much he could actually do for her. "I'll make coffee," he told her.

Another sound, indecipherable this time.

He headed for the kitchen, dragging his fingers through his hair. Guilt gnawed at him. Had he taken advantage of a woman who was drunk? Hell, the thought never occurred to him in his half-awake state. She'd been so eager, so damn willing. And it had been so damn long.

He found the can of coffee in the refrigerator and poured a generous amount of grounds into the coffeemaker, then filled the pot with water.

Cliff had told him to expect a surprise. Had the real surprise been on Cliff's girlfriend?

Bryant swore. He would never knowingly so much as flirt with his brother's girl. They'd made a pact way back in high school. He sure as hell hadn't intended to break it last night.

If he had.

But Cliff's girlfriend surely would have realized

her mistake. Despite the fact they were twins, Bryant and his brother weren't all that much alike. Even in the dark.

Unless the woman was drunk out of her mind. Which she hadn't seemed to be.

But women did screwy things, Bryant admitted. His ex-wife, for one. She'd gone out of her way to trap him into marriage, claiming she was pregnant with his kid. Not so, as it turned out. Their marriage hadn't exactly been made in heaven, but he'd wanted it to work, wanted the kid—until he learned the guy who'd really gotten Diane pregnant had had a change of heart and wanted her back along with their baby. Bryant had let her and the baby go after an attorney made it clear he didn't have a paternal leg to stand on.

The whole episode had left him leery of women, wary of marriage and pretty well convinced, in some way he couldn't fathom, that he didn't deserve a family.

The mugs were above the coffeemaker, and he got a couple of them down, one of them rainbow colored and the other announcing Surf's Up. No doubt the latter was a new addition to the collection.

He wondered what Blondie's story was. He sure as hell didn't want to get mixed up in a mess like he had with Diane again.

"Hello," she called from the other room.

"Yeah?"

"Could you, uh, bring me my clothes? I think they're, uh, in the living room."

He glanced in that direction. Like a trail of bread crumbs, clothing was strung from the front door to the bedroom. He grinned. Anxious lady, whoever she was, and she'd brought her suitcases, too. Maybe she'd been planning to stay awhile—with Cliff.

"I'll get 'em."

"My, um, glasses, too."

He picked up the panties first, a skin-colored wisp of silk. Bunching the fabric in his fist, he closed his eyes. Lovemaking like they'd shared couldn't be a mistake. Unless she was his brother's girlfriend.

Swearing softly, he snatched up the rest of her clothes and her glasses from the end table. He knocked on the bathroom door. She cracked it open an inch or two and stood behind the door so he couldn't peek. But he could see the swell of her hip in the mirror behind her and the graceful curve of her spine. He remembered just exactly how she'd fit in his arms, and his groin tightened at the memory.

"Here you go."

A delicate hand with polished nails and no wedding ring took the clothing. "Thank you." The door closed.

Polite morning-after manners. Must be how they do it in L.A. "The coffee's about ready."

"I really can't stay. Thanks, anyway."

"No need to rush off." He had a few questions he'd like answered.

"Late to work. Sorry."

Late, my foot! She was getting the hell out of there as fast as she could. That could only mean trouble. Bryant and his brother might live a couple of thousand miles apart for the moment, but they were close. Kids growing up on a ranch learned to rely on each other. With twins, that reliance was doubly strong. No woman, even one as sexy as sin, would ever come between them. Bryant, older and wiser than Cliff by a full ten minutes, wouldn't let that happen.

In the kitchen, he poured himself a cup of coffee, straight and potent like he was used to.

Blondie came out of the bathroom, stopping at the bedroom door as though she were afraid he was going to jump her bones. Except for being a little pale, she was neatly put together. Her blouse tucked into a narrow waist, her slacks looking no worse for wear for having spent the night in a heap on the living room floor. He let his gaze wander over her, lingering here and there as he remembered their night together and thinking her big, round glasses made her look studiously sexy. He liked her better naked.

"You feeling okay?" he asked.

"I have a headache. I found the aspirin in the medicine cabinet." She edged into the room, still looking like a rabbit who was about to split.

"About last night," he repeated.

"It was a mistake."

"That's what I figured."

She inched toward her suitcases. "I'd like for you to forget it ever happened."

"Honey, that'll be near impossible, but I'll do whatever it takes to put you at ease."

"Thank you." She exhaled audibly. "I'm sorry."

He lifted his shoulders. What was he supposed to do now? His body wanted to drag her back into the bedroom and make love to her all over again. His head knew better. "You got a car or something?"

"Uh, no. I came in a cab."

"I'll call you one." He reached for the phone book.

"There's a pay phone down the block."

"This will be quicker." She looked unsteady on her feet, as if a good breeze would knock her over. And he didn't particularly want her hanging around a street corner chatting with his brother's neighbors. He dialed the number he found in the book and gave the dispatcher the address. "He said ten minutes."

She sank heavily onto the upholstered arm of a recliner by the French door that led out to a small yard. "I've never done anything like this before."

"What? Get drunk? Or have sex with a stranger?"

She gave a little shake of her head, shifting her hair right where it brushed her shoulders. "Not one of my smarter moves."

"No harm done."

Lifting her gaze, she studied him through the big lenses of her glasses. Cornflower-blue eyes, he realized. "No, no harm done," she whispered.

Something about the resignation in her voice tugged at him. "I don't have a disease or anything like that." He frowned, realizing in a moment of panic they hadn't used a condom. "You don't either, do you?"

Her lips curved ever so slightly, making him wonder how a real smile would soften and change her appearance. "You're safe."

Turning, he poured a cup of coffee for her. "While you're waiting," he said as he crossed the room.

"Thanks." Wrapping her fingers around the mug, she took a sip. Her eyes widened. She choked and coughed, her eyes tearing. "Good grief! Are you trying to poison me?"

He chuckled. "Guess it's a little strong, huh?"

"Strong?" Her voice cracked. "That'd remove the lining of an iron stomach."

"Sorry. We need that kind of fuel to get us through long Montana winters. I guess I've gotten used to potent."

"You must be some cowboy to drink that stuff every day."

She did smile then, a smile that put a sparkle in her eyes like the sun glistening off a high mountain lake. In spite of what had happened last night, Bryant concluded that his brother was some lucky man. He had no intention of telling Cliff otherwise, although he was damned curious to know—

A horn honked outside before he could ask the question he wanted answered. Or maybe it was his sense of guilt that prevented him from asking the question.

"Your cab." Bryant hefted her suitcase. There was a corner of silk fabric sticking out the side, and he had an urge to stroke it, to see if the cloth was as smooth as the woman.

She picked up the smaller carry-on and tried to take the suitcase from him. "I can manage."

"I always see the lady out," he told her. "It's a sort of Code of the West thing."

Color staining her cheeks, she glanced away. "I'm really sorry about all of this."

"Life goes on."

They walked out to the sidewalk in silence, and Bryant handed off the bag to the cabby, who stuck it in his trunk.

"Well, Blondie, I guess this is it. I don't suppose you'd like to tell me your name."

"Not really."

He shrugged. "Your choice." If she was his brother's girlfriend, they'd probably meet again. Which would be quite an occasion, though not one he was necessarily looking forward to.

"Thank you for your understanding." She hesitated a moment, then extended her hand.

She was too soft for Montana, too citified to live on a working ranch where the women got as callused as the men. That didn't prevent Bryant from wishing things could be different, wishing that this woman didn't already belong to his brother.

"See you around," he said, as he held the cab

door open for her. He reached for his wallet to pay the driver, but she waved off the gesture.

Once inside, she raised her hand in a final good-bye, and the taxi pulled out into traffic.

Bryant cursed low and succinctly. Damn sibling loyalty!

LEANING BACK in the cab, Ella closed her eyes and let a shudder ripple through her. She could not imagine feeling more mortified. She'd been such a fool. How could she have done something so entirely out of character? So stupid!

Dear heaven, she'd never be able to face Cliff again. She didn't have the foggiest idea of what she'd say if he called. Not that there was much chance of that.

Surely Bryant realized that she had intended to make love to Cliff, not him. When the two brothers got together and compared a few notes, they'd figure out who had been sleeping in the wrong bed. Or the right bed with the wrong man.

God, they'd probably get a real laugh out of her stupidity.

And then she'd never hear from Cliff...or Bryant again. Which she richly deserved.

A sob caught in her throat and she blinked back the press of tears. To her amazement, it was Bryant, not Cliff, she regretted never being able to see again. No one else could have claimed her virginity with such gentle caring, and he hadn't even been aware of the boon she'd been asking of him. And the morning after, under the most bizarre circumstances she'd ever been in, Bryant had been a true gentleman.

She imagined he was wondering if that was how all the women in California behaved. No doubt he'd hightail it back to the ranch and warn Cliff to stay away from the oversexed, faithless females in those wild beach towns he'd heard about.

The cab reached her apartment, several blocks from Cliff's place and farther from the beach. Gratefully, Ella paid the driver and climbed the steps to her unit on the second floor. The aspirins, which had only marginally helped her hangover, were wearing off. She needed more pain pills, a long soak in the tub, and a major case of short-term memory loss.

BRYANT SPENT the afternoon strolling along the beach, enjoying the warmth of a spring day in Southern California. Pretty little fillies in skimpy bikinis sashayed past him trying to attract his attention, but the only bikinis he could think about were the ones that Blondie had been wearing.

Not a good direction for his thoughts to wander, he told himself.

Whatever she'd been up to, she was history. For Cliff's sake, he'd never admit to meeting her. To knowing her… Intimately.

Except he'd noticed she had a tiny little mole on her left buttock, which he would dearly love to kiss. And the way her nose turned up ever so slightly made her look sassy and cute, in spite of those big glasses she wore. For a woman who'd been caught naked with the wrong guy in the wrong bed, she'd displayed considerable poise.

Yet somehow he suspected she hadn't been all that experienced. An amazing, almost impossible thought, considering what they'd done together.

IT WAS GETTING on toward dinnertime when five-year-old Stevie came racing into the house.

"Unka Bry! Unka Bry!" The boy launched himself into Bryant's arms.

"Hey, bucko, how's it going?"

"I learnt to swim at grandma's house."

"That's great, kid. You're getting to be a real old salt, huh?"

"No, I'm gettin' big."

Laughing, Bryant hugged his nephew hard against his chest. It had been a real tragedy when Cliff lost his wife in a car accident, but at least he still had Stevie. Bryant tried not to be too envious that *he'd* been denied the family he'd always wanted.

Cliff sauntered into the house through the back door, grinning, and opened his arms for a brotherly hug. "Son of a gun, took you long enough to come visit."

"Hey, Bro, the big city's not exactly my thing. And that freeway's a killer."

"It is sort of like an unending stampede, isn't it?" Cliff said wryly.

Lowering Stevie to the floor, Bryant glanced past his brother's shoulder to the back door, half expecting to see Blondie waiting there patiently to be "introduced."

The doorway was empty.

"So, Bro, what's your surprise all about?" Bryant asked as Stevie raced down the hallway to his room. The kid never *walked* anywhere.

"It's great news, that's what."

If it's about the woman in your bed, I already know the best part.

"Sheriff Colman called last week. He's planning to step down as county sheriff next year and he wants me to run in his place."

"Sheriff?" Bryant's jaw went slack with surprise.

"Hey, what's wrong? Don't you like the idea?"

"No, it's a great idea. Really. You'll be terrific and Reed County needs a guy like you. It's just that—" He dragged his fingers through his hair, not sure whether he should be pleased or disappointed that Blondie wasn't part of his brother's surprise. "When you said you had a surprise for me, I thought maybe it was something personal. Like you found yourself a woman or something."

Cliff looked at him stunned, even a little hurt. "Not me, at least not in L.A. Not a one of the women I've met could handle our blizzards. Nothing 'round here 'cept city girls and sunseekers. Not our cup o' tea."

Bryant figured that was true. But it left him wondering who the hell the woman was who'd slipped into Cliff's bed last night. Where had she come from?

As far as he knew, she could still be Cliff's girl-friend, a woman who didn't realize what little chance a city girl had of hog-tying his brother into marriage. Whatever the case, Bryant didn't dare ask too many questions.

He could never admit he'd slept with his brother's woman.

And confessing he'd slept with a total stranger who'd dropped by the house didn't seem like a smart thing to do, either.

"Come on, Bro. Let's have us a beer." He looped his arm around Cliff's shoulder. "Let's have a toast to the next sheriff of Reed County." *And to the woman who's going to haunt my dreams for a long time to come.*

Chapter Three

Six weeks later

A touch of food poisoning caused Ella to be late for work Monday morning. It must have been the chicken she'd had last night. And on Saturday night she'd gotten into some bad strawberries that upset her stomach on Sunday morning. Or maybe the cantaloupe she'd eaten had been overripe.

Whatever the problem, she wasn't looking forward to her day at the office.

Marcie Jackson, the store credit manager, buzzed her in through the security door to the cash room, and Ella headed for her cubicle. Drained did not begin to describe how lousy she felt.

"Hey, hon," Marcie called after her, following Ella into her office. She was a large woman with a friendly smile that masked a penchant for being the world's biggest gossip, although always in a kindly fashion. "I saw a friend of yours this weekend."

Ella wasn't much interested. "Really?" She stashed her purse in the lower drawer of the file cabinet and turned to check the messages on her desk. Not many, thank goodness.

"Yeah, you know, that hunky guy you dated a couple of times. He's a cop or something. With that really cute little boy?"

Ella's head snapped up, which did a number on her irritable stomach. "Cliff?"

"Yeah, what a charmer." Marcie plopped herself down in the chair in front of Ella's desk and it groaned, objecting to the woman's sudden weight. "Me and my sweetie were at the beach, see? Just sunning ourselves, you know? And this beach ball comes bouncing right smack into the middle of our picnic lunch. Knocked over our drinks. Made a real mess."

Ella muttered a response, but she wasn't exactly interested in Marcie's story. For the past—how long had it been…six weeks?—Ella had done all she could to put the *incident* out of her mind. She hadn't talked to Cliff. Didn't plan to. She was far too embarrassed.

Lord, how could she have been so stupid?

"Anyway," Marcie continued, "the ball belonged to Cliff's kid. What a cutie he is. An' they were at the beach with this real nice lady—the kid's teacher, I think they said. Anyway, Cliff gave us a couple of extra sodas he had in his ice chest. Wasn't that nice of him?"

"Very." Curiosity got the better of her. "Was he, well, dating the teacher?" The moment she asked the question, Ella wished she'd bitten her tongue instead.

"Looked like it to me. But it might be they just happened to show up at the beach at the same time. You know how that happens sometimes."

Ella did, and she'd been avoiding the beach nearest Cliff's house for the past several weekends. No way did she want to run into him. The mere thought caused her stomach to roll one more time. She really needed to get something to calm her indigestion.

"She's real pretty, that teacher."

"That's fine." Reaching for the phone, Ella tried to put an end to Marcie's gossiping. "Look, I've got quite a bit of work to do. Can we talk later?"

"Sure. I just thought you'd want to know. In case you wanted to call him, or anything."

Not likely.

When Marcie finally left, Ella sighed with relief, taking off her glasses and rubbing her eyes. She didn't want to call Cliff. She didn't even want to think about him.

Or his brother.

Forgetting the phone call she was going to make, she leaned her head in her hands, waiting for another wave of nausea to pass.

Six weeks since the *incident* and she was still so mortified by what she'd done, she could hardly bring herself to drive past the street where Cliff lived.

Six weeks...and she'd been sick two days in a row. In the morning. She hadn't had her period since...

Her mind shifted through the possibilities, suddenly rejecting food poisoning as the cause. Or a case of the flu. Which left her with…

Morning sickness.

''Oh, God…'' she groaned. No, it couldn't be! Nobody did it just once and got pregnant. It wasn't fair!

Except her sister had claimed when she got pregnant with little Melissa that she was as fertile as a rabbit.

Maybe Ella was, too. Maybe fertility ran in the family.

SHE MADE IT through the day—barely—her stomach settling down after she had some chicken noodle soup and crackers for lunch. On the way home from work, she stopped at a drugstore. She still couldn't bring herself to believe she was pregnant. The idea was ludicrous. Nobody could be that unlucky.

Not that she didn't want children. She did. Three or four would be perfect.

But she wanted babies to come along *after* she'd found a husband, not before. In that regard, she was as old-fashioned as her parents.

For a brief moment as she stood looking at the assorted pregnancy tests lined up neatly on the drugstore shelf, she wanted to sneak one into her purse so no one would know.

So her parents wouldn't know.

They'd given Tasha such a hard time about her unintended pregnancy before her first marriage. Prior to that her parents had even criticized Tasha about the number of dates she'd had in high school. Ella had never wanted to be on the receiving end of their disapproval in the same way her sister had. She'd strived so hard to be perfect. Above reproach.

Tears clogged her throat so tightly, she could barely breathe. They'd be so disappointed in her. The *good* daughter. Daddy's little angel.

Yeah, right!

As though she were a criminal, she averted her eyes when she bought the test kit and paid for it in cash. No paper trail. No one would know what she'd done if the results were negative.

Except Ella…and Bryant Swain, assuming he hadn't mentioned the *incident* to his brother.

Closing her eyes, she pictured him standing in Cliff's bedroom, his body stark naked and decidedly aroused. Deep down inside, her body responded with a force that shocked her. She wanted him.

"Oh, shoot…"

She snatched the kit away from the clerk before the poor girl could even put it in a bag, and she marched out of the store to her car. There was only one way to get past this. To get Bryant Swain out of her mind.

Once home, she didn't even stop to check her mail. Instead she went directly to the bathroom.

The test will be negative, she mentally chanted like a mantra. Food poisoning could happen to anyone. Even a woman who'd done something really foolish.

So could pregnancy, she discovered minutes later

when a big pink plus sign appeared on the plastic tube. Shoving her glasses up her nose, she blinked, hoping that the pink neon mocking her would vanish.

It didn't.

Her whole body began to tremble. She bent over nearly double and was sick again.

What in heaven's name was she going to do?

She couldn't call Cliff and say, "I know we're only friends—or used to be until you started dating someone else—but I've got this really big problem. I slept with your brother by mistake and now I'm pregnant. Would you mind marrying me so I don't shame my parents?"

A hysterical laugh broke from her throat and immediately turned into a sob.

Sitting on the cold tile floor, she pulled her knees up to her chest and tried to figure out what to do. Oddly, she didn't question for a moment that she wanted this baby, would keep it at any price. But because of her family, making the decision to raise the baby on her own didn't come easily.

She needed a husband. Soon.

Cliff was out of the running. She couldn't burden him with another man's child, even his brother's, when it had been her foolish mistake that had caused the problem. Cliff had his own life to lead, which he was only now getting together after the death of his wife two years ago.

No, she couldn't ask him for that big a favor.

Idly, she ran her finger along the grout lines that

separated the blue floor tiles. How would Bryant react to a marriage proposal? she wondered.

He was divorced, she knew. Cliff had often talked about his twin brother, whom he idolized. And it was clear Bryant's brief marriage had not been a happy one, though Ella hadn't learned the details.

Surely he wouldn't be thrilled at the prospect of a marriage to a total stranger. Well, a stranger except in the most intimate of ways.

Still, he was a good man. An honorable man, according to his brother. A true gentleman, as she'd seen for herself.

Montana. Was it worth the trip? Would he be willing to consider a temporary arrangement? A marriage in name only, for the sake of the baby?

At the very least, Bryant deserved to know he had fathered a child even if he elected not to take responsibility for an error in judgment that was entirely her own. She certainly wouldn't blame him if he chose that course. Most men would, she imagined.

Allowing the memory of their night together to surface, she recalled how very gentle he'd been with her. A big man, he could have overwhelmed her with his strength. Taken her fast and hard without recognizing her inexperience. But his coiled restraint and tightly reined power in the face of his own aroused passion spoke volumes about Byrant as a man. As a lover.

Removing her glasses to rub a niggling headache at her temple, she considered the wildest possibility of all. That Bryant and she were meant for each other. That fate had intervened in the lives of two people capable of great love. That they could find that love together.

For a woman who dealt in columns of numbers, interest rates and overdue accounts on a daily basis, that was a fanciful idea.

That she could love Bryant Swain.

And he could love her.

But as she prepared for bed that night, the idea wouldn't let her go. In terms of probabilities, it was definitely a long shot.

But it was a gamble she had to take.

THE SCENT OF RAIN was in the air, freshening the breeze. To the northwest, the clouds were building over the peaks that marked Glacier National Park in the northern corner of Montana. Some years the seven-thousand-foot pass through the mountains wasn't clear of snow until after the Fourth of July. And here on the prairie, snowfall was common as late as June.

Sitting astride his gelding as he studied the approaching weather, Bryant pulled up the collar on his sheepskin jacket. Looked as if it would be a cold June for the cattle they'd finished branding this week and moved to the summer range.

He tapped his heels to the horse and reined him toward home. A snow this late in the year wouldn't be deep. His cattle, still shaggy with their winter coats, would be able to find plenty of the new grass that had turned the landscape to a fluorescent green.

And the calves were plenty old enough to keep up with their mamas, assuming one of the Canadian wolves the feds had reintroduced into the national park didn't take it upon himself to wander outside the boundary in search of an easy meal.

When a man's livelihood was at stake, it was hard to appreciate nature's predators.

He didn't much appreciate the human predators, either, the ones who had taken to rustling twenty head of cattle at a time from adjacent ranches, using a big rig truck and trailer for their getaway. So far they hadn't hit the Double S. But Bryant and his hired hands had to keep a good lookout.

The town of Reilly's Gulch was ten miles south of the Double S ranch. From a rise of ground, Bryant could just make out the glow of lights from the small community, like a single candle in the gathering twilight.

L.A. had been a whole lot different. It never got dark there. Not even in the dead of night. And the stars hardly ever showed, at least not in the millions like a man could see in a Montana sky.

Idly, he wondered if Blondie had ever been to Montana.

Or if Cliff would bring her home with him as his bride next year when he returned to run for county sheriff.

His fingers tightened on the reins, and the horse danced sideways.

"Sorry, fella, I wasn't thinking about you."

Maybe if she'd given Bryant her name, he could have gotten her out of his mind. But Blondie stuck there like a needle in a broken record on that old crank-up player at the line shack on the west boundary of the Double S, an A-frame cabin that doubled as a fishing camp. Over and over the record kept playing *Blondie, Blondie*. And he couldn't forget how she'd felt in his arms. How he'd felt inside her.

Pulling his hat low on his forehead, he heeled the gelding into an easy trot. No sense to be out here in the cold when the storm hit. That was when a man ought to be at home sitting in front of a warm fire.

Or in bed with a sexy woman.

SHE'D GOTTEN LOST twice just getting out of Reilly's Gulch. Didn't these people believe in street signs?

Of course, the narrow roads could barely be called streets, much less highways, and there were no lights at the intersections, even if there had been a sign to read.

Highway was a terrible misnomer, but that was what the locals called them.

She'd had no trouble getting directions to Bryant Swain's ranch, just following them.

The old geezer at the gas station had been more than willing to tell her where the Swains ranched, along with a colorful history of who had settled the adjacent ranches in the 1800s and exactly where their offspring—through three or four generations—now lived.

Ella grinned. My gracious! She hadn't known

people like Arnie with his slow drawl and whisk-
ered cheeks actually existed outside of old westerns.

But wandering aimlessly along dark, country
roads was not a good plan, she realized. The moon
had vanished behind a cloud some time ago, and
the air coming in the window of her Mazda Miata
had a decided chill to it. This was June, for
heaven's sake. She'd expected summer weather, not
the cold of winter.

Another mile or two and she'd turn back. In
Reilly's Gulch she'd spotted an old building with a
hotel sign swinging in the breeze. The accommodations weren't likely to be luxurious, but she could
at least hope for clean. Tomorrow, in the light of
day, the Double S would no doubt be easier to find.

She shivered a little, worried about the reception
Bryant Swain would give her. She might well be
on a fool's errand.

She was almost past the arching ranch entrance
when she noticed the elaborate double S's made out
of wrought iron stretching across a narrow dirt
drive. She swerved to make the turn. Too late.
Overshooting the target, her car plunged into a gul-
ley at the side of the road, slipping hubcap-deep
into the mud among a stand of pussy willows and
mashing the right fender into a granite boulder.
She'd barely missed hitting a mailbox perched on
a wrought iron post in the process.

"Oh, shoot..." she muttered.

That was when the first drops of rain spattered
onto her windshield.

She shoved the gear into reverse and tried to back

out of the quagmire. It was a no-go. The front wheels just dug in deeper. She was well and truly stuck.

Gripping the steering wheel to steady herself, she drew a deep breath. She hadn't seen another car since she left Reilly's Gulch. It was growing quite late and the air was cooling by the minute. If she was going to get help, it wouldn't come from someone who just happened along this deserted road.

It would come from the Double S. From Bryant.

But the ranch house wasn't in sight.

"How far can it be?" she rationalized. In upper New York, farmhouses were in shouting distance of the road. How different could Montana be? True, she'd driven through long stretches of highway where there hadn't been even a glimmer of habitation.

But this was his driveway. It had to lead to the house, which couldn't be all that far away.

From the back of her car, she hefted her shoulder bag with overnight necessities, leaving the heavier suitcases until later, and found her denim jacket. In ten minutes walking time she'd be there. How wet could she get in this gentle spring rain?

BRYANT HEARD the sprinkles change to a heavier rain and then the hail came, pounding down on the land, mashing the new grass and bouncing off the tin roof of the back porch like a drumroll. He reached over to close the window above the kitchen sink. It was a good night to be home.

Mollie, his aging collie, whined and stretched.

She didn't go out much anymore, preferring the comfort of a warm kitchen in winter and a cool front porch in summer. On arthritic legs, she trotted toward the front door.

"What is it, girl?" Bryant frowned. Over the pounding of the hail, he detected the faint sound of knocking. Nobody used the front door, not in this part of the country, except maybe a process server. So far as he knew, nobody was suing him. And this was sure a rotten night to be serving papers.

He thought about Diane and shook his head. That divorce, and all the associated details, were long over.

Mollie whined again, this time with more emphasis.

A cautious man, Bryant grabbed a shotgun on the way to the front door and cradled it under his arm. This might not be Los Angeles, but crazy things happened out here, too, and his hired hands were all in the bunkhouse.

He switched on the porch light and opened the door.

Shivering in the cold air, a five-foot-five-inch drowned rat stood before him, with wet hair plastered to her head, jeans and a denim jacket soaked through from the rain. A woman who looked strangely familiar, and who was carrying a small suitcase over her shoulder.

His mind couldn't take it all in. Who the hell—

"Bryant? Could I…c-come in?"

"Yeah, sure." He opened the door wider, and as she stepped inside he glanced out into the dark night to see if she was alone and how she had gotten here. No one was in sight.

She stood in the entryway, dripping water onto the hooked rug by the door, Mollie sniffing at her curiously.

"My c-car got stuck. It was f-farther from the r-road to the house than I expected."

"You walked?" It was a good two miles, and in this weather...

Nodding, she pulled a pair of glasses from an inside pocket and slipped them on, looking up at him with cornflower-blue eyes.

Recognition slammed into him like a bull on a rampage. "Blondie!"

A slight smile curved her lips. "My name's Ella...Ella Papadakis." Another shiver went through her.

"Come on." Quickly propping the gun in the corner, he took the bag from her and headed her toward the kitchen where he could get some hot coffee into her. Questions could come later. "We've got to get you warmed up." He guided her down the hall, his hand at her waist, and he remembered with uncommon clarity the last time he had seen her. And how much he'd wanted to make love with her again.

"Let's get that jacket off," he told her, helping her out of the wet denim. Her blouse clung damply to the outline of her breasts, the fabric nearly see-through, her nipples beaded by the cold. "Your shoes and pants need to come off, too. As soon as

I get the coffee going, I'll get a robe for you to put on."

"I'm sorry to show up like this."

He busied himself at the counter, filling the coffeepot, trying to ignore the tactile memories that flooded his body, his primal response to her.

While the coffee perked, he hurried upstairs, grabbed his robe from the hook in the closet and snatched a towel from the rack in the bathroom, surprised by how hard his heart was galloping.

She murmured her thanks when he returned, her gaze not meeting his.

Still shivering slightly, she rubbed her hair with the towel, then turned her back to discard her blouse and pull on the robe before dropping her jeans to the floor. The robe came nearly to her ankles and was big enough to wrap around her almost twice. Her feet were bare, slender with faint tan lines from wearing sandals.

He couldn't stop staring at her. Why was she here?

"I must look a sight," she said when she turned back to him.

"You look fine." His voice thickened in his throat. Except for an occasional cleaning lady, there hadn't been a woman in his house for five years. Not since his ex-wife left.

Gesturing toward the kitchen table, he said, "Sit down. I'll get you some coffee."

Pulling the robe tightly around her, she did as he suggested. She looked small sitting there, and vulnerable.

"I'm not actually supposed to have caffeine."

His hand hesitated on the pot. "How come?"

"I'm pregnant."

For the length of a full minute, the room was dead silent, neither of them so much as breathing as he absorbed what she had said.

Then the rage came from somewhere deep in his gut, suddenly rising like a lightning bolt, burning him with blue heat. Rage that had been festering there since his ex-wife left him, taking with her the hope of the family he'd wanted, the baby that he'd held in his arms and had learned to love. Another man's child.

His jaw muscle flexed, and he forced himself not to ball his hands into fists. "That doesn't have anything to do with me."

She went very still, looking vulnerable as though she'd been slapped. What color she'd had in her cheeks drained away. "I didn't mean to tell you like this."

"Tell me what?" He didn't give a damn. This time he wasn't going to listen.

She licked her lips and pressed them together. "That night... You're the baby's father."

"You really expect me to believe that?" He'd gotten the same lies from Diane, and he'd been a damn fool to believe her. To want a family so much, he even thought he could love his wife.

"I wouldn't lie to you. Not about something as important as this."

He barked a sound that was close to a curse. "Yeah, right. That's what all the women say."

Folding her hands in her lap, she gazed at him steadily. She didn't so much as flinch at his harsh tone.

"I came here because I thought you had the right to know you're going to be a father. I had hoped..." Her gaze slid away from his.

"Hoped what? That I'd pay support for some kid who probably isn't even mine?" What kind of a fool did she take him for? They'd slept together once. And it had been *her* idea, not his.

"No, I don't need your money. I was hoping, for the sake of your child, you'd be willing to marry me. Temporarily."

He gaped at her as if she'd lost her mind. Or he had. Two women pulling the same stunt on him? God, he must have Sucker stamped in capital letters on his forehead.

"No way, Blondie. You can just get on your horse and ride back the way you came. I'm not going to fall for that line again. Not in this lifetime."

Chapter Four

She'd handled this poorly.

Ella didn't know how to take back her words or the abrupt way she'd broken the news of her pregnancy to Bryant. Little wonder he didn't believe her.

How did any woman diplomatically drop a bombshell like that in a man's lap? Particularly when she barely knew him.

In the face of his anger, she said, "I'm sorry. I guess I made a mistake by coming here."

"You've got that damn straight. You're real good at making mistakes, like spending the night in a stranger's bed."

Inwardly, she cringed. "Actually, I managed to go twenty-eight years without making a mistake as big as that one. And then only after I was almost killed in a plane crash, and I decided that I shouldn't die a virgin."

He lifted a skeptical brow.

She ignored his reaction, determined to get through this confrontation with a minimum of embarrassment. "I drunkenly decided to ask a favor of a friend—your brother. We were only platonic friends—"

"You sure as hell knew where he slept. And you had a key."

"That's true, but only because I fed his fish when he and Stevie were out of town."

He shook his head in disbelief.

"I also knew Cliff was a nice guy. Unwisely, I thought he'd be happy to rid me of my virginity. So I climbed into his bed. Except Cliff wasn't there. You were."

"That's crazy. No woman is stupid enough to—"

"I was."

"But you admit you thought it was going to be Cliff in that bed."

She nodded. "We'd sort of talked about—"

In two strides, he'd reached the opposite side of the kitchen table. He leaned toward her, his palms planted firmly on the table and glared at her. His expressive eyebrows flattened into a straight line. "Do you have any idea how I felt knowing I'd slept with my *brother's* girlfriend? My *twin* brother's girlfriend? Damn it, I crossed a line Cliff and I swore we'd never cross."

"It isn't as if your brother and I had any kind of an understanding. Sleeping with you—" Had been wonderful, the most glorious night of Ella's life. "—just happened. You can blame fate, if you'd like."

"Oh, no." He shook his head in disgust. "I blame myself. *And* you."

"I'll accept as much of the blame as you care to give me. I couldn't have been more foolish if I'd stepped out in front of an oncoming train." Although, at the time, her misstep had caused her more pleasure than pain. "But I should point out in my own defense, *you* were in that bed, too."

He backed away and shoved his fingertips in the hip pockets of his jeans as though he were afraid he might hit someone if he didn't keep his hands under control. His wide-legged stance thrust his pelvis out, and like an auditor in search of evidence of past misdeeds, Ella's gaze was drawn to the worn fly on his pants, to the bulge there. Memories assailed her, sending a shudder of awareness through her.

Swallowing hard, she forced herself to look away.

Outside, the rain was still coming down hard, drumming on the roof and splashing against the window. The collie who'd been lying beside Ella stretched and nuzzled her hand. Automatically, she petted the dog, smoothing her hand over the animal's grizzled muzzle.

"She must be old," she said almost to herself.

"Mollie's nearly fourteen. When she was young, she used to help with the roundups. She'd do the work of two hired hands." His voice softened with pride and affection, wrapping itself around Ella as warmly as his old robe. "She's got arthritis now. Can't do much but sleep and eat."

But Bryant hadn't gotten rid of the dog when she was no longer useful, Ella noted. That spoke well for him, of a certain nobility and compassionate nature.

"How badly did you damage your car?" he asked.

She was grateful for the change of topic. "I don't know. The front wheels are hubcab-deep in gunk, and I probably whacked a fender. The motor still runs."

Glancing outside, he said, "No sense to try to pull you out in this weather. You can use the spare room for tonight. In the morning, I'll haul you out of the ditch and you can be on your way."

For a moment she couldn't breathe, the ache in her breastbone so painful, it was as if she had taken a blow to her chest. He was rejecting her…and her baby. Ella had hoped to have more time to convince him of the possibilities, of why—for the sake of the baby—they should at least try a marriage in name only.

But she'd rarely had much success in attracting a man. Bryant was no different. If he'd gotten a good look at her plain-Jane features before they'd made love, he probably would have tossed her out of bed, too.

Shoving her glasses up her nose, she lifted her chin a notch. "I don't want to put you out. If I can use your phone, I'll just call the auto club."

"Blondie, the nearest auto club tow truck comes from way the hell in Great Falls, and on a good day it'll take him three or four hours to get here. Assuming he makes it at all in this rain, chances are good the driver is some sixteen-year-old kid with an attitude, and he's guaranteed to yank your bumper right off the car. You'd be better off to wait till tomorrow.''

''Very well.'' She stood with as much dignity as she could, considering she was wearing a terry bathrobe several sizes too large for her and had very little on underneath. ''I appreciate your hospitality.''

''We westerners are known for our warm welcome.''

She arched a brow.

''Of course, it can't compare to your welcome in California. That was one hell of a night.''

Heat flooded her cheeks. At least he hadn't forgotten that night.

Nor had she.

HE SHOULDN'T have put her in the bedroom across the hall.

Stacking his hands beneath his head, Bryant stared up at the ceiling above his bed. Not that he could see anything except what was in his imagination.

Blondie. Her hair spilling across the pillow.

Blondie. Her lips slightly pouty, ready to be kissed. Her eyes vulnerable.

Blondie. Naked and waiting for him.

She'd said she'd been a virgin.

Groaning, he rolled onto his side and punched his fist into the pillow. Her name was Ella. Ella

Papadakis, she'd said, and she was pregnant with his child.

It couldn't be. A scam, that was what she was pulling. He couldn't even know for sure that she was pregnant. Hell, she hadn't looked pregnant when she showed up at his door, not in those rain-soaked, shrunk-to-fit jeans.

That night in L.A. she'd intended to sleep with his brother. But Bryant had been there instead. Without giving his brother much thought, he'd made love with Blondie. Enjoyed it. A lot.

He didn't know which was worse, his guilt that he'd slept with his brother's girlfriend or that he'd carelessly taken a woman's virginity without even being aware of what he was doing. But he did remember how tight she'd been, her soft cry of surprise when he'd entered her.

Yeah, assuming she really was pregnant, and assuming she hadn't slept with any other guys in the past couple of months—including his brother—he could be the father of her child. If that was the case, he had to take responsibility for his actions.

But he didn't have to be railroaded into marriage to a woman who happened to stumble into his bed. He'd been down that path once and didn't plan to go there again.

ELLA'S EARS strained to hear the night sounds.

After the rain stopped, a profound silence settled across the land so that each individual sound gained more significance. A wolf howling in the distance. A cow lowing closer at hand and the soft nicker of a horse. Wood creaking as the house shifted with the changing temperature. The sound of a man turning restlessly on his bed across the hall.

The press of tears stung at the backs of her eyes, and she slid her hand protectively across her midsection.

Bryant wasn't going to marry her. The thought that he might actually agree to any kind of marital arrangement with her had been as foolish as having slept with him in the first place.

She used to be so levelheaded. She wondered what had happened to her. Now she'd have to raise the baby alone. And she'd have to tell her parents their "good" daughter was a fallen angel.

It seemed as though she'd just managed to nod off when a noise woke her and she sat up with a start, momentarily disoriented. Then she remembered where she was. And why.

With a sigh, she threw back the covers, put on her glasses and went to the window, lifting the curtains. What she saw took her breath away.

The rolling landscape drifted away toward the horizon in a sea of vivid green that was almost more than her eyes could absorb. Occasionally an oak or willow tree or outcropping of rock added emphasis to the scene like an exclamation mark.

In contrast, the cloudless sky was so brilliant a blue, it was like being inside a painted glass dome. The air was thick with the scent of grass and wildflowers, and somewhere an unseen meadowlark called to its mate.

No wonder Cliff had been eager to return home

and Bryant remained on the land. Ella was half in love with the place already and she'd only seen a tiny portion of Montana.

Stepping out of her room wearing the oversize bathrobe, she discovered her jeans and blouse neatly folded beside the door. She smiled to herself. A cowboy who knew how to do laundry, too.

After using the bathroom down the hall, she dressed quickly and headed downstairs. It was a big house with four or five bedrooms upstairs, a house built for a family, not a single man living alone. The thought of filling those bedrooms with babies—Bryant's babies—left her a little breathless.

She stopped midway down the stairs, resting her hand on the solid oak banister. So much of her life would change now with the baby, starting with finding a place to live larger than her cramped apartment when she got back to L.A. Her throat tightened on the thought that she couldn't stay here. She'd been so full of hope that she was doing the right thing by coming to Montana. By seeing Bryant again.

But she'd been wrong.

She found him in the kitchen, standing at the stove. He turned to look at her, his gaze shifting over her in the same way it had on another morning, the morning after they'd made love. His hair looked rumpled from sleep, the unruly sandy-blond strands drifting down over his forehead. Barefoot, his shirt was unbuttoned and hung open, revealing the breadth of his chest; rolled-up shirtsleeves exposed bare arms roped with muscles. Everything about him radiated sex appeal—the intensity in his eyes, the fullness of his lips, clear down to his lean hips.

Her senses reeled with the impact he had on her.

Dear heaven, in all the confusion of last night, in the face of her being so wet and cold, and Bryant being so angry, she hadn't realized the real reason she'd come to Montana. Not because of the baby. Not so that she wouldn't embarrass her parents or herself.

But because Bryant Swain was the only man who'd ever made her feel like a woman.

She desperately didn't want to give that up.

"You want pancakes for breakfast?" he asked. Fine lines radiated from the corners of his eyes, as though he spent a lot of time squinting into the sun, and his face and neck were deeply tanned, darker than his chest. "Eggs and bacon?"

"Plain toast for me, thanks. And herbal tea, if you have any."

He raised his brows in a way that suggested real cowboys didn't drink tea at all, much less the herbal variety.

"I've had some trouble with morning sickness," she told him. "Nothing serious, but I have to go kind of easy on my stomach till lunch or so."

He studied her with an appraising eye. "You don't look pregnant."

"I'm only about eight weeks along. I won't show till four or five months."

"You're really pregnant?"

"The doctor confirmed it."

"And I'm..."

"The father, yes. But it's entirely your choice how much involvement you'll have with the baby," she hastened to add. "Or with me."

His body language told her he wasn't too thrilled with either prospect.

"One slice or two?" he asked, opening a cupboard over the counter and pulling out a loaf of bread. The kitchen looked like it had been remodeled in the last ten years with new oak cabinets, tile counters and modern appliances—a kitchen a woman could enjoy.

"Let's start with one slice. No sense to press my luck."

"You got it." He dropped a piece of bread into a four-slice toaster.

"Aren't you eating?"

"I did. Hours ago. Normally I'd be out checking the herd by now or working the fences, but it seemed inhospitable to go off when you were still sleeping."

She checked the clock on the stove. It was only six-thirty. That was a half hour earlier than she normally got up to go to work.

He didn't have any tea so she settled for some apple juice, which she thought wouldn't upset her stomach.

As he had last night, he sat down opposite her at the table with a cup of coffee while she nibbled on her slice of dry toast.

"So," he asked a little too casually, "do you have a job in L.A.?"

"If you're wondering if I'll be able to support

the baby, the answer is yes. I've got a good job with plenty of fringe benefits.'' She just didn't happen to have a man like Bryant around, a man who made her stomach do twirly things that didn't have anything to do with morning sickness.

Lust, she thought. It had to be lust and long-term celibacy. But she couldn't quite make herself believe that. Her feelings were too deep, well beyond primal, though objectively that made very little sense.

''You've always, ah, lived in L.A.?''

Ella got the distinct feeling she was getting the third degree. Bryant's cop brother would be proud of him.

''I'm a New Yorker by birth, raised in Queens by a family that wrote the textbook on traditional family values. My company transferred me to the West Coast last year. It was a promotion.'' A significant raise in both pay and responsibility that she'd been eager to accept, particularly since the idea of living some distance from her overly protective family had seemed like a good one at the time. But she hadn't enjoyed the work as much as she had expected. Playing the role of villain to customers who had gone too far in debt wasn't a whole lot of fun.

''Papa…dakis?'' He struggled with the pronunciation. ''Is that Greek?''

She grinned. ''I can make baklava blindfolded. It's a rite of passage for all young Greek girls.''

The smile that creased his cheeks did devastating things to her, making her heartbeat accelerate at a frightening rate and sending curling warmth through her midsection. Dear heaven, this man must have every woman in a nine-county area trying to land him as a husband. Ella didn't have a prayer.

"I've never tried baklava. What's it like?"

"Mouthwatering. Once you've tasted it, store-bought cookies won't cut it anymore."

He seemed to focus on her lips for a moment, then abruptly downed the last of his coffee and shoved his chair back from the table. "Let's see if we can get your car unstuck. I'm sure you're eager to get back to L.A."

She wasn't. Not at all. But it was beginning to look like she didn't have much choice.

She hadn't been able to see much of the ranch last night in the pouring rain. Now as she left the house with Bryant, she discovered several well-kept outbuildings, a brightly painted red barn and a stable. A cowboy wearing chaps and looking as if he'd answered a Hollywood casting call was working a horse in the corral while another man stood by the fence watching the rider. From what she could see, the Double S was a prosperous business enterprise.

"Does Cliff live here, too?" she asked.

"Nope. He and his wife built a house on the section closer to town. She liked being near her family, and Cliff needs to be closer to the action."

"Action?"

"Highway accidents. The usual Friday night ruckus at Sal's Bar and Grill. All that crime stuff sheriff deputies have to worry about."

"Hardly the makings of a crime spree in either New York or L.A."

"True enough. That's what gives him the time to lend a hand during our busy season, like round-ups. We're partners in the ranch, but I handle the day-to-day operations."

From all she'd seen, he'd managed everything quite well.

As they approached the barn, she caught the earthy scent of hay, manure and leather mixing in an aroma that was both potent and appealing in a primal way. Very masculine. Just as Bryant was more totally male than any man she'd ever met, a combination of great genes and living in a rugged environment.

The cowboys at the corral noticed Ella, stopped what they were doing, their heads swiveling in her direction.

The heat of a blush stole up her neck. What must they be thinking? Or was it usual for Bryant to have a woman stay overnight?

"Hey, Rusty," Bryant called to the man standing at the corral.

"Yeah, boss." He shoved away from the fence and sauntered toward them. Tall, wiry and bowleg-ged, he had the walk of a man who'd spent years riding a horse. Lines mapped his face, and Ella would have guessed his age to be somewhere be-tween sixty and eighty years old.

"Ms. Papadakis went off the road in the storm last night," Bryant said. "I'm going to have to haul her car out of the ditch."

Grinning, Rusty lifted his hat, revealing a fringe of curly carrot-red hair circling a bald dome. He looked like the victim of an inexperienced poodle groomer who'd had a bad accident with her shears and a bottle of dye. "Sorry you had a problem, ma'am."

She returned his smile. "Luckily I wasn't far from the ranch house. Mr. Swain generously offered his hospitality." If Bryant could be formal, so could she.

"You jes' passin' through, ma'am?"

"She's on her way home," Bryant answered for her. "To Los Angeles."

"Now there's a real pity, I'd say. Could use a pretty little thing like you around here to spruce up the place. Too many bachelors and not 'nough womenfolk, if you want to know the truth. And some of them there bachelors get real cranky when they don't—"

"Rusty!" Bryant interrupted. "When Pete finishes with that cow pony, I want you two to go up to the north section. I thought I saw motorcycle tracks up there. I don't want some kid tearing up the sod, you understand?"

"Yes, sir, I surely do." His watery blue eyes twinkled. "And if the lady decides to come a-visiting again, she can jes' let me know. We'd be glad to fix her up with accommodations in the bunkhouse."

"That's very sweet of you, but I think—"

Bryant took her by the arm, propelling her toward a four-wheel-drive pickup parked beside the barn. "Sorry about that old goat. Rusty hits on any woman under the age of ninety, but he's harmless."

"I think he's charming."

"I'd stay clear if I were you." He tossed her bag in the back of the truck. "Sal at the local honky-tonk has had her eye on him for years. She doesn't take well to competition."

He opened the passenger door and Ella started to get in, which turned out to be more of a problem than she had anticipated. She had to step way up, and she couldn't quite find anything to grab on to to pull herself up.

While she was struggling and feeling a little foolish, Bryant's big hands closed around her waist. Heat rocketed through her as he turned her, then lifted her up onto the seat. Startled, she held onto his rock-hard forearms. He didn't immediately let go, and they were eye to eye. Tremors rippled through her. Her mouth went dry. For a moment, open lust burned in his eyes, darkening them to a navy-blue, and she knew her eyes must reflect the same needy desire.

She wanted to celebrate. She wanted to clap her hands and cry out that he wanted her in the same way she wanted him. But before she could speak, he did.

"Next time, try using the step. That's what it's for." His voice was rough and sharp-edged, cutting off her earlier thought that he desired her at all.

He let go of her. She glanced down, feeling the fool once again. "I didn't notice."

"Yeah, well, I noticed your nice derriere, Blondie. It's not a real good idea to waggle it around in front of a cowboy. You never know what might happen.''

He slammed the door in her stunned face. What on earth—

And then she smiled. As compliments went, it was the best one she'd ever had. He liked her butt. She almost wept at that small victory.

BRYANT NEEDED the full five minutes it took to reach the highway to get himself back under control.

First she'd thought his old goat of a foreman was *charming,* and then she'd waggled her sweet little rear end right in his face. In an instant, his body had gone hard, his jeans losing a couple of sizes, and he wanted to take her right there on the front seat of the truck.

Dumb idea.

Dumber still that he'd wrapped his hands around her, that he'd touched her and let all those memories of making love to her come roaring back.

She'd been a virgin.

He had to get her to her car and on her way before he did something really stupid, like ask her to stay. She'd satisfy the cravings of his body, but she'd play mind games with him, too. Diane had. The rules had all been stacked in her favor. It had been lose-lose for him.

He reached the highway and pulled up behind her car. She managed to get out of the truck on her own. Perversely, he was sorry she hadn't needed his help.

"That's it," she said. "Well and truly stuck in the mud."

He shook his head, studying the small Mazda Miata convertible. Not only was the car stuck, she'd come close to clipping his mailbox, too. "Blondie, in these parts we don't call that a car. It's a windup toy."

"It is not," she said, affronted. "It's a perfectly good car, sporty, and the first one I've ever owned. People don't need cars in Queens."

"It wouldn't survive the first snowfall around here." It had barely made it through a spring rainstorm.

"You'll remember, I live in Los Angeles. We don't have much snow there."

"Lucky for you and your car."

She gave a careless toss of her head that started her hair swaying. He fought the urge to snare her, to bury his fingers in her hair and draw her mouth to his.

Instead, he edged his way into the ditch, the mud oozing up to his ankles, to study how much damage she'd done to the front end of her car. Except for a banged fender, it didn't look too bad.

He had a motorized winch on the front of his truck, good for hauling mired cattle out of the mud or stumps out of the ground. A compact car presented no problem at all. Except there wasn't much room for him or anyone else to snake under the car to hook the business end of the winch to the axle.

He'd never make it unless someone lifted the rear end off the ground by about a foot.

He eyed Ella skeptically. A city girl, all right, her jeans sporting a designer label. Except for running them through the dryer last night, they looked brand-spanking new. Her silky blouse was wrinkled but little the worse for wear considering the drenching it had taken last night.

"What is it?" she asked.

"How do you feel about getting that fancy outfit of yours dirty?"

She looked down at herself as if she were surprised he thought her clothes were anything out of the ordinary. "You're supposed to get jeans dirty, aren't you? What do you need me to do?"

Need and want were two different things, Bryant reminded himself. Wants you could do without.

"I'm going to lift the rear of your car. You're going to crawl underneath and hook up your axle to the winch."

Her eyes widened behind her glasses. "You're going to *lift* my car?"

"Only one corner of the rear end. It's not very heavy. It probably weighs less than a heifer."

"A toy, right? So you keep saying. But what if you drop it on me?"

"I won't."

She seemed to measure his answer for a moment, or his resolve, then nodded. "No, I don't suppose you would."

That she trusted him so easily gave him an odd feeling. Not that he doubted his own strength. But she didn't exactly know him real well. She could have refused, told him to find someone else. Sent for the damn auto club. Instead she'd agreed, in effect, to put her life in his hands. And the life of her child.

Sweat broke out on Bryant's forehead. *She was carrying* his *child.*

He reeled off the steel cable and handed the hook to her. "You know what an axle looks like?"

"I think I can figure it out."

He hoped so. He didn't want her lingering under there playing eenie-meenie-minie-moe with weak struts that wouldn't hold up when pressure was applied.

Positioning himself at the rear corner of the car, he asked, "Ready?"

"Whenever you are, Cecil."

He frowned. "Who's Cecil?"

To his dismay, she laughed, a warm, languid sound that swept over him like a hot summer sun. "A movie director, probably the greatest of all time. Go for it, Cecil." She lay down on the ground in the dirt and high grass at the edge of the road, not the least worried about her clothes, and grinned up at him. "And keep the cameras rolling."

His legs went weak and his mouth went dry as he lifted the car and she squirmed under it. God, she had a sexy body. Breasts a man wanted to hold in his palms. A flat stomach. Hips made for making babies. Long, strong legs.

"Don't hang around under there too long," he

warned, sweat dimpling his forehead and edging down his neck.

"Coming."

She scooted back into view, and he was treated to the sight of the buttons on her blouse having popped open. Her bra was flesh-colored and lacy. *Just like her bikini panties had been.*

Breathing heavily, he dropped the car.

"So? You still think this little baby is a toy?" She came to her feet as easily as a champion rodeo rider thrown from a bull.

"I think you need to stand back out of the way while I haul your car out of the mud," he said gruffly.

She moved away, her bright spirit subdued by his harsh words, while he set the winch in motion. The Mazda inched back onto the road.

"Poor baby," she murmured. "I'm sorry I clobbered you."

Bryant walked around the car, then lay down to examine the underside. It didn't take him long to discover Ms. Papadakis wasn't going far anytime soon.

Standing, he brushed the dirt from his hands.

"I guess I can be on my way," she said far more cheerfully than he would have liked. It didn't seem right she was so eager to get away even if that was exactly what he wanted, too. "Thanks for all your help—"

"Not so fast. You've bent the steering rod. This car isn't going anywhere except at the end of a towing cable. I'll take you to the closest garage."

Chapter Five

"*Four* days?" Ella gasped.

"Yes, ma'am." Arnie at the Reilly's Gulch Garage ran his thumbs underneath his overall straps. "Might be a sight longer if the auto parts supplier in Great Falls ain't got the right part for this here funny little car."

She gritted her teeth. "It's *not* a funny little car."

"I remember I had me an MG in here once what needed fixin'. Fellow was from See-attle, kind of a young guy—"

"Arnie, the lady's only worried about her own car," Bryant said. "Can we stick to the subject?"

"Sure I can. But it ain't gonna make that there steering rod get here any faster if I do."

"Would you mind calling Great Falls?" she asked, making the effort to keep her voice pleasant, the tone she used when dealing with a disgruntled customer. "Perhaps there's a way they can expedite shipment."

"If they got one."

"Of course," she said.

Bryant tapped the toe of his muddy boot in an impatient rhythm as though he were as upset about the delay as Ella was. She had a reason to want to linger in Montana. He wanted her to leave.

"If you got the part tomorrow," Bryant asked, "could you get the car fixed by the end of the day?"

"Nope."

"Why not? How long can it take—"

"The UPS truck don't make it to Reilly's Gulch till nigh onto four o'clock. It'll take me two, three hours to pull the old rod out and put the new one in. That'd take me past suppertime."

Ella rolled her eyes. She certainly wouldn't want Arnie to be late for supper.

"I always take my Saturday-night supper with the Widow Carson." Arnie's grin suggested he took some other liberties with the widow on Saturday night. "The next day being Sunday, I don't work none."

"Everyone needs a day off," Ella commented.

"Yes, ma'am. That'd be true."

Bryant said, "So you could fix her car on Monday."

"If I get the part."

"Right." Bryant thumbed his hat farther back on his head. "Arnie, why don't you call your supplier and see what he can do for you?"

Finally convinced to make the phone call, Arnie ambled into the garage office; Ella and Bryant waited outside.

An abandoned railroad track divided the Reilly's

Gulch business district, such as it was. Old warehouses, now unused, stood next to the track along with a building housing the Cattlemen's Association. Then came a small brick building with gold lettering proudly announcing that it played a dual role in the community both as city hall and the Reed County courthouse. The school was at that end of town, too—home of Reilly's Ranchers—and two big yellow school buses were parked out front, waiting for the schoolchildren to return from summer vacation.

At the commercial end of town near Arnie's garage, Ella could see a grocery and dry goods store, a combination beauty-and-barber shop, and a feed store. A sign in the upstairs window above the feed store announced that the *Reed County Register,* a weekly newspaper, was published from the second-floor offices.

Dining choices in the small community appeared to be limited to Reilly's Diner or Sal's Hotel, Bar and Grill, neither of them on any five-star lists, she imagined. Indeed, there was a rather strong odor of greasy hamburgers in the air which nearly masked the sweet smell of sage blowing in from the surrounding rangeland.

On the outskirts of town near a small, white clapboard church, she'd noticed a sign that claimed a population of 582 for the town, but the number two had been crossed out, replaced with a zero. Not exactly a booming population and a long way from Queens or L.A., but the town had a rugged western feel that Ella found refreshing.

An old Buick with rusted fenders and door panels cruised down the street at ten miles an hour. A man pumping gas waved to the driver and a woman coming out of the grocery store across the street did the same. Friendly town, Ella concluded.

Bryant, leaning back against his truck, had found something interesting to study in the dirt at his feet while they waited for Arnie. With his Stetson shading his eyes, Ella couldn't read his expression. The broken car part had given her a reprieve to stay a while longer in Montana, but she didn't sense he was pleased.

He raised his head, meeting her gaze. "How come you waited so long to…you know…make love?" he asked quietly.

She hadn't expected him to be thinking about that. "To please my parents, I guess. Not that I had all that many opportunities to, ah…you know." This was definitely a difficult subject to discuss, particularly out here in the open.

"You mentioned that Cliff said he would—"

"I think he was joking." Embarrassed, she glanced away.

"But he's the one you picked."

She shrugged. "I didn't have a lot of choices."

He reached out as if to touch her, then let his hand drop to his side. "The guys in L.A. must be blind."

She couldn't enjoy the full measure of his comment because Arnie chose that moment to return.

"You're all set, ma'am." He was wiping his hands on a blue grease rag. "Had to call all the way to Cheyenne, but I found us the part, all right. Not too much call for them particular steering rods 'round here, not for them little dinky cars.''

"Fine. Then you can have my car ready by Monday?"

"'Fraid not, ma'am." He stuck the rag in the back pocket of his overalls. "It's two-day delivery from Cheyenne, so the rod won't get here till Monday. But I'll have yer car right as rain come Tuesday. And that's a promise, ma'am.''

Bryant said, "Sounds like she'd be better off if I drove to Cheyenne and picked up the part myself.''

"You're welcome to, if that's what you want, boy. But I still couldn't get the work done till Monday.''

Ella waved off Bryant's suggestion. "One extra day won't matter.''

"You don't have to get back to work?"

"I took an unpaid leave of absence. I didn't have any more vacation time coming." By not quitting her job outright, she'd hedged her bet just in case her trip to Montana had been a bust. She'd obviously lost her wager.

His eyes narrowed. "But you do have a job to go back to?''

She nodded, her throat thick with the bitter taste of disappointment. She had a job; he didn't need to worry about supporting her or the baby. Or ever seeing her again.

Digging deep for control, anticipating the worst when she had to tell her parents the news of her impending maternity, she turned away. "Thanks, Arnie, I'll pick up my car on Tuesday," she said over her shoulder. "I'll just get my bags now. Sal's Hotel ought to have a room—"

Bryant's hand snared her by the arm. "You can't stay at Sal's."

She looked up at him in surprise. Lord, he was a big man. "Why not?"

"Well, because…" His deeply tanned complexion took on a reddish hue. He glanced over his shoulder to be sure Arnie was out of hearing distance. "Because sometimes when the cowboys come to town, they bring a girl with them. Or maybe they meet somebody in the bar. Then they…"

"Use the rooms upstairs?"

"You're getting the idea."

"Well, they won't burst into my room, will they?"

"Probably not. But these guys who come into town on a Saturday night can get pretty drunk. It's hard to say what they'll do. And you're sure not likely to get much sleep."

The walls between rooms in a building that old had to be paper thin. "I'll be fine."

Squaring his jaw, he said, "No, I'll take you back to the ranch."

"I appreciate your willingness to sacrifice on my behalf," she said tautly, "but surely there's somewhere else—"

"It's not a sacrifice, okay? And, no, there isn't anywhere else to stay in Reilly's Gulch." He took the keys from her hand and headed to the back of the car. ''I'll get your bags.''

''I'll take a bus to Great Falls.''

''We don't have bus service here.'' He pulled her suitcases from the trunk and carried them to his truck, tossing them into the back.

''Someone can give me a ride. I'll hitchhike.'' She didn't want to force herself on him, not when he didn't want her. And it was clear he thought inviting her back to the ranch was about as much fun as chewing on cactus. In fact, he was just that prickly.

''Don't argue with me, Blondie. Get anything else you need out of that car of yours and let's get going. Some of us have a ranch to run.''

Bryant got into the truck and slammed the door shut behind him.

No way did he want her hanging around Sal's. Not that he'd expect her to do anything all that awful, not if she was left to her own devices. But she was too beautiful for her own good and the guys who hung out at Sal's wouldn't be adverse to taking advantage of a woman as innocent as Blondie.

He ought to know. When he'd been testing his oats as a kid, he'd had a few memorable evenings there himself.

His pa had tanned his hide good when he'd found out.

Once Ella was in the truck, he gunned the engine, but had to wait for Chester O'Reilly in his old

Buick to pass before he could pull out into the street. He waved to him and got a nod in return.

"Who's that man?" Ella asked. "I just saw him going by the other way a minute ago. Everyone seems to know him."

"Chester O'Reilly. His grandpa founded the town. Old guy is pretty bored since his sons took over running the feed store. He drives around town all day just checking on things. Sort of a self-appointed Neighborhood Watch."

"Maybe someone ought to give him something to do so he'll feel useful again."

Bryant shot her a look. He didn't want Blondie to get involved with the town or his neighbors. She wouldn't be staying long enough to care.

Four days. He gripped the steering wheel tightly and made a left onto the street. He'd have to keep his hands off her for four days and keep his hunger for her at bay for four long nights.

ONCE THEY ARRIVED at the ranch house, he left her on her own, escaping to the comfort of his cattle, Ella thought. She changed into a clean pair of jeans, found the washing machine to do up some laundry and wandered outside.

The air was warm and dry. Puddles of rainwater that had formed during the storm had already evaporated, and the heat of the overhead sun would soon draw the rest of the moisture from the ground.

From the few clouds building in the distance, she suspected the cycle might soon start all over again.

As intrigued by the ranch as she was by its

owner, she decided to investigate the outbuildings. She headed first for the stable.

Inside, sunlight slanted through half-open stall doors, creating a checkerboard effect of light and dark. Dust motes danced in the air like a late season snowfall. Bits of straw decorated the dirt floor, and the pungent odor of animals and wet dirt formed a rich blend of earthiness.

A horse stretched its neck over the edge of its stall, nodding a welcome and nickering softly.

She approached cautiously. "Hi, fella. Would you let me pet you?"

He blew her a big-lipped kiss.

"I hope that's a yes," she said, laughing.

His nose was like velvet, his breath warm on her hand. She scratched him along the length of his nose and then between his ears.

"You know, the last time I petted a horse, it was in Central Park and I was about five years old. I remember begging my mother to buy me a pony. I was sure our backyard was plenty big enough." She chuckled at the memory. The closest she'd come to owning a horse had been a huge collection of plastic ones which she played with constantly, often to the exclusion of her equally large collection of Barbie dolls.

Bending, she picked up a few wisps of hay. The horse took her offering, his soft lips just brushing her fingertips. "Maybe I can find an apple or carrot for you later. Would you like that, fella?"

"It's a girl, ma'am."

Ella started at the sound of a masculine voice.

Turning, she found a young cowboy strolling toward her. "Oh. I didn't even think to check."

"Yes, ma'am. Her name's SusieQ."

"Well, SusieQ seems like a fine horse to me."

"The boss bought her to breed with Archer, his stallion. Come spring next year, she'll have a foal that'll be worth plenty."

Ella would have her baby by then, too. Bryant didn't seem exactly thrilled by that prospect.

"You a friend of boss, ma'am?" the boy asked. He looked to be about sixteen, still troubled by acne and not yet fully grown, though she already had to look up to him.

"A friend? Something like that." She wasn't sure there was an official title for someone who was a stranger yet was about to be the mother of a man's child. "Why don't you call me Ella. I've been called ma'am so much since I got here, I'm beginning to feel ancient."

"Yes, ma'am." His face turned beet-red and he curved the brim of his hat, tipping it. "Ella."

"And your name is…"

"Shane. Shane Connolly. I'm one of the hired hands 'round here." He said it so proudly, Ella couldn't help but smile.

"Well, Shane, since you're here, do you suppose you'd be willing to do me a favor?"

"Oh, yes, ma'am—Ella. Happy to do whatever I can for a friend of the boss."

"Does Bryant have a nice gentle horse you think I could ride? Just around in the corral?"

"Uh, well, I guess."

She gave him her most encouraging smile. ''I'd really appreciate it. You see, ever since I was a little girl, I've wanted to ride a horse and I've never had the chance. It would be a special treat for me.''

The boy hesitated and stammered a bit but finally decided a friend of Bryant's ought to be treated to a horseback ride as long as she was visiting the ranch—assuming she'd stay in the corral and let him hold the halter, guiding the animal until she caught the hang of things. Grinning, she was more than happy to agree to his restrictions.

He picked out SusieQ as being the most suitable horse for Ella, and she watched in fascination and growing excitement as he saddled the horse, holding her steady while Ella prepared to mount.

Smiling to herself, Ella decided the trip to Montana wouldn't be a total waste after all.

Shane cupped his hands, Ella grabbed the saddle horn, and he boosted her up onto the seat.

''Oh, my!'' she gasped, delighted. ''This is really high up here.''

''Let me fix those stirrups for you, ma'am.''

She didn't even object to being called ma'am again. She was simply too excited to worry about feeling old.

He led SusieQ out of the barn and into the corral, giving Ella a few basic riding instructions while still keeping the horse under tight control. She tried to absorb everything—the feel of her butt rocking in the saddle, the stretch of muscles to accommodate the animal's girth, the creaking of leather. Even the view from her mile-high perch. She was giddy with childish enthusiasm. Like having sex, she wondered why she had waited so long.

She spotted Bryant striding toward the corral and waved, her grin almost painfully wide.

With sparse effort, he climbed the fence, and marched across the riding ring toward her. "What the hell do you think you're doing?"

"I'm riding a horse. Isn't it great?"

Shoving Shane out of the way, Bryant grabbed the horse by the halter. "Get down."

"I'm not hurting your horse, Bryant."

Shane said, "I made sure she was real careful."

Ignoring the boy, who was quickly retreating to the far side of the corral, Bryant said, "Have you ever ridden before?"

"Well, no, but Shane had SusieQ under control. And I wasn't exactly planning a cross-country trip."

"Has it occurred to you, Blondie," he growled between clenched teeth, "that given your delicate condition you might hurt yourself?"

She gaped at him. Was he worried about *her?* "I'm not an invalid, Bryant. I'm perfectly healthy. I do aerobics three times a week. Exercise is *good* for my condition."

"You could fall. Or be thrown."

She rubbed the horse's neck. "SusieQ and I have an understanding. She isn't going to throw me."

He closed his eyes and blew out a sigh. He'd overreacted. He'd seen Ella up on SusieQ and he'd panicked. Visions of her falling off, being trampled, had caught him by surprise and he'd had to stop her, to protect her. And the baby. *His* baby.

A baby he couldn't be a hundred percent sure was his and didn't want to care about for fear he was setting himself up again for a fall.

"Indulge me, okay? Just get down off of there and we'll talk about it."

She shrugged, her radiant smile dissolving into disappointment. "It's your horse."

Releasing the reins, she grabbed the saddle horn and swiveled to dismount. Instinctively, he reached for her. His sudden movement and her shifting weight unsettled SusieQ, who sidestepped away, which threw Ella off balance. She fell back into his arms with a startled cry.

"I've got you."

His arms wrapped around her. He could feel her heart beating hard against his palm, smell her faint wildflower scent. Her hair brushed against his cheek, strands catching on his collar. The softness of her rear end settled into the nest of his hips, and he bit back a groan.

Damn, how could she do this to him when he wanted her gone? When he didn't want to remember how it had been that night. When he wanted to forget he'd made love with his brother's girlfriend—however platonic the relationship had been—and gotten her pregnant.

He steadied Ella, then let her go.

Looking up at him through those big glasses of hers, she smiled wryly. "I guess I forgot to ask Shane a few details about getting off a horse."

"Yeah, a few."

"You won't yell at him for letting me ride, will you? It was my idea. He was reluctant, but I talked him into saddling SusieQ for me."

Bryant suspected she could talk her way into almost any kind of mischief with a smile like that. "I won't yell at him."

He went after the horse, picking up the reins that had dropped to the ground, then handed the mare over to Shane with orders to put her back in her stall.

Ella had waited for him.

"Shane seems like a nice boy," she said as they walked toward the house.

He shortened his stride so she didn't have to run to keep up with him. "He's a good kid. From Chicago. A runaway."

"A runaway?"

"Yeah. City kids get this crazy notion that they all want to be cowboys. Things get tough at home and they head west. Some of 'em end up here."

"And you take them in?"

She made it sound like he was running a Boys' Town. He wasn't. But the Swains had adopted Bryant and his twin when they were five years old and given them a loving home after they'd been abandoned by their mother. This was his way of returning the favor, helping other kids who needed a boost up.

"I put them to work. They find out for themselves punching cattle isn't all fun and games. Then

I drive them to Great Falls and give them a bus ticket home.''

"How long has Shane been here?"

He thought for a minute. "About a year now, I think."

"And you're letting him stay?"

"He doesn't have anywhere else to go. I made him call home about a month after he got here to let his folks know he was okay. The phone had been disconnected. His letters came back stamped No Forwarding Address. From what he's said, I'd guess his parents were glad he left."

"He idolizes you, you know?"

He shrugged, letting her walk up the back steps ahead of him. Over the years, some of the strays he'd taken in had figuratively kicked him in the teeth. Others, like Shane, he could feel good about.

He slid a glance at Ella, wondering if she'd be like Diane and kick him when he was the most vulnerable, when he thought he was starting his own family. If he kept his distance, if he didn't care about her or the baby, it wouldn't hurt so much this time. That was how he intended to handle the situation.

She stopped at the screen door. "Bryant Swain, has anyone told you lately that you're a real softy?"

"Not lately." He fought to suppress a grin. Fought not to respond to her warmth and friendliness. "And don't spread that rumor around. It'll ruin my reputation with my hired hands."

She laughed as she went inside, the sound as joyous as a songbird's call on a spring morning on the prairie. He desperately wished he could take a risk with a woman like Ella. But not under these circumstances. He'd left himself vulnerable once. He didn't intend to do it again.

ELLA HEARD his alarm the next morning.

Squinting at the bedside clock in the guest room, she concluded getting up at four-thirty was uncivilized. Nonetheless, she struggled to her feet and pulled on her jeans. Everyone else worked on the ranch. She might as well make herself useful, too.

Tail wagging, Mollie greeted her in the kitchen. After a few good-morning pets, the dog wanted to go outside. Ella followed her onto the back porch and got her first look at a Montana sunrise.

Some unseen hand had dipped a brush in a rouge pot and painted the eastern horizon the color of a rose garden. Radiant streaks of gold shot upward, turning the gray of predawn into day. Even as she watched, the sky changed to pale blue, the vivid colors of sunrise erased by morning's arrival.

"Oh, my," she sighed. "A girl could get used to living here." Not that she'd been offered a chance.

Turning, she discovered Bryant standing at the back door watching her. Her heart stumbled on the unfamiliar intimacy of sharing a sunrise with a man. *With Bryant.*

"Good morning," she said, her voice husky with emotion and needs she tried not to think about. "It's going to be a beautiful day. Montana is the most incredible place I've ever been."

"Summers can be blistering hot," he warned, "and the mosquitoes grow the size of B-1 bombers. Then the grass turns tender dry. One spark and a wildfire can scorch everything in sight. In winter a man can freeze in ten minutes and be buried under a foot of snow within thirty."

He was doing his best to warn her off, to spoil the mood created by the beautiful sunrise, but she wouldn't let him. "Then when we get a day like this, we ought to enjoy it."

He eyed her dubiously. "Have you always been such an optimist?"

"Nope." She edged past him into the house, catching a whiff of his natural masculine scent, a base note among the fragrances of dawn. "Montana brings out the best in me. What do you want for breakfast?"

"You don't have to cook for me."

"Sure I do." Looking back at him, she grinned and shoved her glasses more firmly in place. "That way you'll feel obligated to take me on a picnic." She could only hope her sometimes queasy stomach would behave itself. She only had four days left to convince Bryant to give her baby his surname.

CLAIMING HE HAD too much work to do, Bryant put off their picnic until Sunday. And as much as she pleaded, he wouldn't take her on horseback. The truck would have to do. Later, he promised, she could ride SusieQ in the corral—with him overseeing her lesson.

His protectiveness was oddly comforting, though she bristled at his domineering ways.

Driving cross-country made for a bouncy trip. The track he followed was only the width of the truck with two ruts and grass growing down the middle high enough to brush the truck's undercarriage. To pass through rocky areas, they had to straddle boulders, and the truck wobbled precariously. Ella held on tight, tempted to point out this ride was far bouncier than anything she'd likely experience on a horse.

"Are we still on Double S land?" she asked after they had driven for some distance.

"You'd have to go nearly twice as far as we're going today before you'd run out of Double S land." With obvious pride, he named the total acreage encompassed by the ranch boundaries.

"Wow. To a New York City girl, that's impressive."

"It's impressive to most Montanans. My great-grandpa staked out this land in the 1870s. He had to fight Indians and squatters alike, but he held on to the land. I intend to do the same."

"It should be easier now. At least no one is shooting at you."

"Nope. But there are still rustlers around. And the price of beef and profit margins keep going down at the same time feed bills and taxes go up." He glanced over at her, his eyes keen with determination. "That's why I was in L.A. I was trying to make a deal for our Cattlemen's Association with a beef exporter for the Asian market."

"Did you?"

He refocused on the narrow track. "The deal's still pending."

From his tone, Ella suspected the deal's outcome was important, not only to him but to the other ranchers in the area. And she felt her own sense of unfounded pride that his neighbors had selected Bryant as their spokesperson.

They passed a turnoff where the rutted trail made a Y.

"What's that way?" she asked.

"A small cabin. We call it a line camp, but Dad just happened to build it close to his favorite fishing hole on the river. Every once in a while, he'd escape up here to do a little fly fishing. When Cliff and I were kids, he'd take us along. It gave Mom a break. And later..." He let the words drift off.

"You were lucky to have such good parents."

He glanced her direction. "Yeah, we were."

Eventually he parked at the edge of a slow-moving river and spread a blanket in the shade of a cottonwood tree, where they sat down at opposite sides, both leery of getting too close. A low murmur of insects played as a counterpoint to the rustle of leaves and the flow of water past the muddy riverbank.

"This must surely be God's country," she said, taking in the sweeping view.

"It can be, yeah. Or the devil's own." He was leaning back against the tree, one knee raised and his Stetson tipped up. There were shots of white in the blue of his eyes, like tiny lightning bolts. His lashes were long for a man, slightly curving. His nose was straight, his lips full and his jaw firm.

She swallowed hard, imagining his handsome features in miniature on the face of a baby. Her baby and his.

Unable to handle the rush of emotion, she reached for the picnic basket to conceal the tears that sprang to her eyes. Her chin trembled. She'd never had much success attracting a man. This time, when it counted so much, she'd failed again.

Keeping herself busy, she filled a plate and passed it to him.

He raised his brows. "Fried chicken? That's not very Greek."

"We're from southern Greece," she said straight-faced.

"And deviled eggs, too." Chuckling, he plopped one in his mouth whole, chewing with obvious pleasure. "My mom used to make those."

"Cliff said your mother died when you were quite young."

"Ten. Cancer." He looked away, though she thought she'd glimpsed tears in his eyes. "That's a helluva disease."

"And your father?"

"Mom dying practically killed him, too. After that, he concentrated on us kids…and the ranch. I think the land was what he loved most." He leaned back again. "After Cliff and I graduated from college and could take over some of the ranch duties, he decided he was overdue for a vacation. He'd taken a Caribbean cruise and was touring some island down there. The tour bus tipped over on a curve.'' He shrugged. ''Dad didn't make it. Maybe after Mom died, he was simply looking for a way to follow her.''

Instinctively, she placed her hand on his arm. ''I'm sorry. They must have loved each other very much.''

''Yeah. When I got married... Well, it didn't work out that way for me.''

Shifting slightly, folding her legs under her, she selected a piece of chicken for herself. ''I knew you were divorced. Cliff never mentioned what happened.''

He bit into a crispy chicken breast and then took a second bite before he spoke. ''I tried to do the right thing and it turned out wrong.''

''Marriage is never easy, I suppose.''

''She told me she was pregnant and that the baby was mine. She said she loved me. She lied on both counts.''

Ella stopped eating her deviled egg in midbite, a troubling sensation raising the hair on her nape. *A lying woman.* Is that what he thought she was?

''She wasn't really pregnant?'' What a cruel trick.

''She was pregnant, all right, but the kid wasn't mine. She had another boyfriend she hadn't bothered to mention. He didn't want to marry her, not then. So she conned me into it instead. And I was fool enough to believe her scam.''

''That's terrible.''

''The worst part was, even after I realized I was

deceiving myself about loving Diane, I still wanted that baby. I took Diane into Great Falls and we stocked up for the nursery. A crib. Stuffed animals. A mobile with teddy bears. I really got into it. And then she had the baby. I held her...Terrilynn.'' His voice broke. ''That's when her boyfriend showed up with a change of heart.''

It was Ella's heart that went out to Bryant. He'd had his hopes dashed by a woman's betrayal. He expected her to do the same ''And when I came knocking on your door with the same story, it was déjà vu.''

''Pretty much so,'' he conceded. ''After Diane left, I talked to an attorney. Legally, since Diane and I were married, Terrilynn was my baby even if I wasn't her biological father. The attorney told me to forget it. Nine times out of ten, mothers have all the rights. So I had to let 'em both go.''

No wonder he'd been furious with Ella that night, more than reluctant to believe her story. Were their positions reversed, she would have felt the same way.

But amazingly, in the case of his ex-wife, he'd wanted the baby to be his even when he realized he no longer cared for the woman. Bryant wanted a family; he'd be a great father as evidenced by his caring for boys like Shane and his eager anticipation of parenthood.

Ella's heart swelled with love for a man who was potently masculine but also good to the core.

Darn it all! Even if Bryant didn't want to marry her, her child deserved to know its father, to know what a wonderful caring man he was. And it was her job to make that happen.

She reached into the picnic basket, selected a caffeine-free soda and popped the top. "I'm not going back to Los Angeles."

"You going home to your folks? That's probably a good—"

"No. I'm staying right here. In Reilly's Gulch."

He looked at her as if she'd grown ears and a forked tail. "You can't do that."

"Why not? I'm over twenty-one. I can live anywhere I want to live."

"But your job's in L.A."

"I'll get one here."

"Doing what? Mucking out stalls?"

"If I have to." She narrowed her gaze and shoved her glasses back up her nose. He didn't have the slightest idea how stubborn she could be when she set her mind to something. He couldn't bully her or boss her around like he did his hired hands. She wouldn't let him.

"I like Montana—a lot. I want my child to grow up in a place where people leave their doors unlocked and don't have to worry about getting mugged or shot at in a drive-by shooting. I want my child to learn how to ride a horse and fish in a stream. So I'm going to stay right here in God's country."

And the fact that deep in her heart she recognized she loved Bryant Swain was an added bonus. She'd stay in Reilly's Gulch as long as it took to get him to love her—and their baby.

Chapter Six

Myriad emotions shot through Bryant, driving him to his feet. *She was going to stay in Reilly's Gulch.*

He stalked to the edge of the bank, whirled back. Memories of his first marriage, of the baby he'd lost, nearly brought him to his knees. "You're trying to force me to do something I don't want to do."

"No, I'm not," she said with irritating calmness. "I'm making this decision because it's what I want for myself and my baby."

"But you think by hanging around you'll embarrass me into marrying you."

"The very last thing I want—" her voice dropped to a whisper barely audible above the purring flow of the river "—is to embarrass you. If you'd like, I won't tell anyone you're the baby's father. No one will know."

No, that wasn't what he wanted. But he didn't want to be tied by marriage to a woman he barely knew, either. A woman who'd been planning to sleep with his brother. Damn, how was he ever going to explain Ella—and the baby—to Cliff? She'd said they'd had no relationship, but she'd had Cliff's key. And Bryant had made love to her in Cliff's bed.

Like a rattler backed into a corner, Bryant wanted to strike out at someone. But he was the real culprit here—he and his stupidity that night in L.A. Next time some naked woman climbed into bed with him, *he'd just say no.*

She wasn't even suitable to be a rancher's wife, not with her fancy designer jeans and silk blouses that made a man want to caress her, stroke her shoulders, cup her breasts through the shimmering fabric. She was too fragile, her hands too soft. She didn't even know how to ride a horse, for heaven's sake!

And the car she drove. That toy wouldn't make it through one summer on the rough roads around here, much less survive a winter.

Of course, that's it! he thought with grim realization.

Taking off his hat, he speared his fingers through his hair. He didn't have to do much of anything. In no time she'd head back home, away from Montana, returning to her own territory. When the sun turned blistering hot, she'd think better of trying to pressure him into marriage. She wouldn't last until winter—which would drive her away for sure if she did manage to hang on that long.

Thank God he'd figured out his smartest course was to accept his responsibilities but keep his distance. He wouldn't get too close to her—or the baby. That way, when she left like Diane had, it wouldn't hurt too much. He could handle that.

"All right," he said. "There's a little house a block off of the main drag in town that's for rent. It's not much but it ought to do for now. I'll set you up there—"

"You'll what?"

"I'll rent the place for you and I'll give you an allowance since you won't be working."

She came to her feet almost as fast as he had, covering the ground between them in a few angry strides. "Not on your life, cowboy. You're not interested in marrying me—even temporarily—to give the baby your name. Well, I'm sure not interested in your version of being a kept woman, either. I'll take care of myself."

"There aren't any jobs—"

Pointing a finger at him, she jabbed him in the chest. Hard. "You don't have any idea how resourceful I can be, cowboy."

If he hadn't been so upset, he'd have laughed at her. She was one tough hombre when she was mad, pound for pound as feisty as a wildcat with its tail caught in a swinging door.

"Okay, Blondie, have it your way. You think you can make it in cow country, you go ahead and try. When you're ready to give it up, come see me. I'll get you a bus ticket home." He made that offer to all the strays he took in. Sooner or later most of them took him up on the deal. A few others—like Diane—kicked him in the teeth instead.

He wasn't eager to find out which option Ella would take.

ELLA WAS still upset and hurt by Bryant's bull-headed arrogance as the end of the week approached. But that hadn't changed her plans.

She had her car back, though the dent was still in the front fender, and she'd rented the house Bryant had mentioned. For now she was "camping out" with a sleeping bag she'd purchased at the dry goods store along with a pot to cook in and a place setting of cheap dishes.

Fortunately, the house came furnished with an old stove and a refrigerator that actually made a few ice cubes buried beneath an inch of frost.

She was tickled pink with her two bedrooms and a yard bigger than any she'd ever enjoyed in her life. She had some scraggly rosebushes to prune, flower beds to fuss over. And every evening she sat on her porch steps to watch the sun set over the distant mountains. God's country, she thought, grinning.

Next week the movers would come with the rest of her worldly possessions, the process arranged by Marcie, who was going to take over Ella's position as West Coast credit manager. Ella was officially unemployed. She was also in trouble with her parents.

"You've *moved* to Montana?" her shocked mother had asked when Ella finally got up the nerve to call home. "We thought you were just there on a vacation."

"It's beautiful country, Mother. I decided to stay."

"But you'd just settled in California. You had a wonderful job—"

"I know, but there are so many interesting opportunities here in Montana." Like raising her baby near its father. "I felt I had to make the move."

"This is so impulsive of you, dear. I can almost imagine Tasha doing something like this, but not you. You've always been so...so steady."

"And boring, too," Ella muttered.

"Dear, is there some other reason you've, well, made this decision in such haste?"

Ella opened her mouth to tell her mother the truth, that she was pregnant and wanted to live near the baby's father. But her courage failed her. Or maybe she was still hoping Bryant would have a change of heart—for the sake of the baby—and marry her.

"It's wonderful country, Mother," she hedged. "I'll have you and Dad come visit soon so you can see for yourselves." Breaking the news of her pregnancy in person might be easier—though Ella doubted that.

"All right, dear. But call often. We worry about you."

"I will, Mother." Guiltily, Ella had hung up, not bothering to mention that the opportunities Montana presented included very little in the way of suitable employment for her.

Which was the next issue she needed to tackle.

She hadn't packed any of her business suits for

her visit to Montana, but then a suit hardly seemed appropriate as job-hunting attire in Reilly's Gulch. And right here at home was where she planned to start her job search. Nice slacks and a neatly tucked-in blouse would be more than sufficiently formal.

Parking her car in front of the feed store, she studied the businesses that lined the street. As Bryant had suggested, the prospects for employment weren't encouraging.

Two hours later, she'd received three solid No's and a proposition from the flirtatious old guy sitting at the counter at Reilly's Diner—which she'd turned down. She hadn't been able to find anyone at the city hall who knew anything about job openings, and the newspaper office wasn't open.

That pretty well left Sal's Hotel, Bar and Grill as her last shot for the day.

Taking a deep breath, and wishing herself luck, she shoved through the saloon's swinging doors.

The air was cool, the smell of hops potent and the sparse lighting an apparent effort to save on the electric bill. It took Ella's eyes a moment to adjust to the murky shadows.

An old-fashioned bar with padded stools and a foot railing reached the length of the room. Behind it, beer advertisements and pictures of buxom women decorated an equally long mirror. At one end of the room a raised platform suggested live entertainment was a regular feature; tiny round tables with plastic tops were scattered around the remainder of the room, leaving only a small space for a dance floor.

At midafternoon there wasn't a soul in sight. Ella didn't doubt for a moment, however, that on a Saturday night this would be a jumping place.

"Hello," she called, strolling toward the bar.

"In here!" came the reply from a room that was off the end of the bar.

Ella made her way around unopened cartons of whiskey and peered into the office. The woman she saw at the desk was as large as any she'd ever met—better than six feet with beefy arms and the shoulders of a football player—and had her eyes glued on a small TV set on the corner of her desk. She didn't even glance in Ella's direction when she stepped into the room. Though Ella didn't follow the soaps, she gathered the woman, whom she guessed to be Sal, was a serious fan.

Ella watched patiently as the series' youthful heroine wept huge silver tears while telling her boyfriend she understood he had to go away for a while—to follow the drumbeat of his own heart. Brave girl...

Eventually the screen went black, credits rolling, swooping violins playing. Only then did Sal turn to Ella.

"That son of a bee isn't gonna marry that poor girl, and her carrying his baby 'n all. Poor little dear." Tears slid down Sal's puffy cheeks. "Ain't that just like a man? The no-good varmints."

"Well, yes, but sometimes there's a—"

Not paying attention to Ella's response, Sal

grabbed a tissue, wiping her nose and blowing it loudly. ''You must be new around here. Most everybody in these parts knows I don't miss my soaps for nothing, not even a fire if it ain't right here in the office.''

''I'm sorry, I... My name's Ella Papadakis—''

''The girl who's been at the Double S? Well, shoot! Rusty told me about you.'' She stood, extending her meaty hand. ''Why didn't you say so, sweetie? Any friend of Bryant's is a friend of mine. Welcome to Reilly's Gulch.''

Her handshake nearly broke Ella's arm. ''Thank you.''

''Rusty said you was about as purdy as a crocus in springtime but that I didn't have to worry. He likes a woman like me with a little more meat on her bones.'' She laughed a deep, rumbling sound that echoed in the room, inviting anyone within hearing to join in the joke.

Heat stole up Ella's neck. ''That was very nice of Rusty to say—about both of us.'' Particularly since Ella had never considered herself in the least ''purdy.''

''He's a good ol' boy, he is.'' Sal sat down on the edge of her desk, crossing her arms. She wore a man's T-shirt with the sleeves rolled up, and her muscles bulged. ''Now then, what can I do for you, Ella P.? You and Bryant need some packaged goods? I can make you a good—''

''Actually, I'm looking for a job.''

Sal stopped in midsentence. Her dark eyes narrowed. ''Is Bryant's ranch in trouble?''

"No, nothing like that. I was just visiting Bryant for a few days." To break the news that he was going to be a daddy, but the announcement hadn't been eagerly received. "Now I've decided to stay on in Reilly's Gulch indefinitely. I've rented the Murdock house on Sunflower."

"That's real interesting." Beneath Sal's gray-at-the-roots brassy-blond hair, Ella detected a high-powered computer brain at work. "Just what kind of work did you have in mind?"

"I'm willing to do anything."

"You ever do waitressing?"

"No, but I'm certainly strong enough to carry a tray of drinks, and I can add well enough to collect the bill."

"Plus a tip."

"I'd hope so."

Sal shoved away from the desk and went back to her chair. "The boys that come here ain't always real polite. How do you feel about some fella grabbing your boobs or pinching your butt?"

"Not thrilled," she conceded. "But I'd say if the guy wanted to avoid a broken wrist, he'd only do it once. I took a class in self-defense some years back. And riding a subway in New York City, a woman picks up a few tricks. They'll learn to mind their manners."

Sal's smile was warm and filled with knowing. "I think I like you, Ella P. Problem is, I can only use an extra girl on Friday and Saturday nights."

"I'll take it."

"You won't earn enough to support yourself, not in two nights."

In search of inspiration, Ella glanced around the cluttered room. Two filing cabinets overflowed with bits of paper, and a shoe box on the chair was stuffed with what looked like invoices.

"Who does your books, Sal?"

"The bills and such?" She barked an unpleasant sound. "I do, if that's what being overdrawn half the time is called."

"My degree's in business with a minor in accounting. I'm a qualified bookkeeper."

"I can't afford—"

"I'll work cheap. To supplement what I earn waitressing for you. I've got my computer arriving next week. I'd be able to set up an entire system for you in no time, something you'll be able to understand and even do yourself, if you'd like."

Shaking her head, Sal said, "I don't know about that last part. I swear, computers could make a woman sterile, all those little electrons flitting around."

Ella swallowed a smile. Given Sal's age, that shouldn't be a problem. And Ella was proof positive her intimate knowledge of computers hadn't adversely impacted her fertility.

"Then I'll just keep your books on my computer at home and bring you the printouts whenever you want to take a look at them."

Sal eyed the shoe box of invoices, shuddering. "All right, you got yourself a deal, young lady.

Two nights a week here in the bar, all the tips you can muster, and doing the books.''

Sal named a price for the bookkeeping service that would just barely allow Ella to make ends meet when added to her waitress wages, and only then because her rent was impossibly low compared to what she'd been used to paying in Los Angeles. But it was a start. Later, maybe, Ella could enlist a few more customers for her fledgling bookkeeping service. Then she'd be able to stay home full-time with her baby.

All in all, it had been a good day.

The fact that she still lacked a father for her baby—and a husband for herself—was simply a temporary setback.

Bryant, who hadn't even wanted her to stay overnight at Sal's Hotel Bar & Grill, would have a hissy fit when he learned the mother of his child was waiting tables.

BRYANT MENTALLY GROANED when he saw Winifred Bruhn's battered station wagon pull up by the barn. The Press placard taped to the windshield was a local joke. She might be the publisher, editor and only reporter for the *Reed County Register*—as well as the president of the school board—but the sign in the window ought to read Nosy Neighbor.

He didn't need her kind of trouble on a Saturday morning, not when it had been nearly a week since Ella packed up her Miata and moved out on her own. He'd tossed and turned every night thinking about her, remembering that one night they'd had together. And wanting a repeat performance.

Maybe he shouldn't have let her go.

Maybe he should have kept her right here on the Double S where he could keep track of her.

But then she would really be driving him crazy. At least this way he didn't catch a glimpse of her cute little derriere when he walked into a room or a whiff of her subtle floral scent.

"Howdy, Bryant." Winifred waved, heading toward the tractor where he was changing the carburetor.

Straightening, he wiped his hands on a dirty rag. "Morning, Winifred. What disaster has hit our fair community to bring you way out here so early?" Or what bit of gossip did she hope to pass along?

"Problems down at the Rocking D." A spare woman of indeterminate age, her narrow nose, drooping eyebrows and thinly drawn lips gave her a perpetually sour expression. Her biggest joy seemed to be in reporting the troubles of others or their fall from grace when she discovered some small blemish on their virtue. "They lost about twenty or thirty head last night."

Bryant didn't like the sound of that. "The rustlers truck them off?" Often it was no harder to rustle a few head of cattle than to bring a truck onto grazing land and round up as many beef cows as they could find.

"Looks like it. The fence was broken and the semi they used left tracks. The sheriff's on it, not that the incompetent fool has solved a crime in these parts in the past ten years. Past time for him to retire.'' Flipping through a steno pad, she found an empty page and readied her pencil. ''You had any losses lately?''

''Not that I can tell. Some of the boys are out checking the fence on the south side this morning.''

She looked disappointed that he didn't have any grist to add to her article. ''How 'bout any other unusual occurrences? Like strangers in the neighborhood?''

''Pretty quiet around here.'' Too quiet, the house strangely empty since Ella had left. Damned if he hadn't liked having breakfast with her and finding her in the kitchen again at night fussing over dinner when he came back after a long day of work. Those weren't things a man ought to get used to, not when the arrangement would only be temporary.

''There was that young woman visiting you for a few days. What was her name?''

None of your damn business. ''I don't think she's part of a cattle rustling ring.''

''Probably not. But she's waitressing at Sal's and I like to get a handle on—''

''She's what?'' Bryant nearly shouted the question.

''Sal hired her…let's see…'' She checked back a few pages in her notebook. ''Papadakis. She's the one who was here, right? From Los Angeles.''

A muscle in his jaw flexed. ''Yeah, she stayed here a couple of days.'' And she sure as hell shouldn't be working at Sal's.

''Well, then, you can fill in a few details about

her.'' She seemed ever so proud of herself for having trapped Bryant into an admission that he knew Ella. ''For instance, is she a close friend? Are wedding bells in the offing? Or since she's from L.A. maybe it's your brother who—''

He snagged her by the arm, urging her toward her car. ''Winnie, one of these days you're gonna poke your nose into somebody's private business once too often and they're gonna poke back.''

''Now wait just a minute, young man. In this country we have freedom of the—''

''You've got the freedom to drive off my property before I throw you off.'' He opened the car door for her. ''I suggest you do just that.''

She sputtered and fumed about him not being able to muzzle the press, but she finally drove away.

''Good riddance,'' Bryant mumbled.

Damn it all! What did Ella think she was doing? Sal's was no place for her to work. The Saturday night cowboys from miles around would be all over her. Ogling her. *Touching* her. They might even try to take her upstairs to one of the rooms.

Ah, hell! He couldn't let that happen. Not to the woman who was going to be the mother of his child.

''Rusty!'' he bellowed. ''We're going into Sal's tonight.'' And they were damn well going to stop this foolishness—for Blondie's own good.

Chapter Seven

Bryant's stomach knotted like a twisted lariat. He still couldn't quite believe Ella would work in a place like this with cowboys crowding shoulder to shoulder, drinking and swearing, the music so loud a man could hardly hear himself think. She had more class in one little finger than this whole roomful of people; she didn't belong here.

He cut Rusty a glance. "I can't believe you didn't tell me Ella was working here."

His foreman shrugged. "You didn't ask, boss."

Squinting through the haze of smoke and jostling bodies, he tried to spot Ella's familiar blond hair. But there were too many couples on the dance floor, too many guys trying to get a drink at the bar.

"You see her, Rusty?"

"Nope. Sal's behind the bar, though. We could ask her."

"We'll sit a while and watch." Bryant didn't want the whole town knowing he was worried about Ella. It was bad enough Winnie had already sniffed out the possibility of a story. If she got wind of why Ella had come to town and printed the story, Ella's reputation would be ruined. She didn't deserve that.

He grabbed an unoccupied chair, carrying it to an empty table along the back wall. Rusty did the same.

"I'll go get us some beers," Rusty said before sitting down.

"Let's wait for a waitress." And hope Ella was assigned the tables at this end of the room.

His foreman eyed him speculatively. "A man can build up a mighty big thirst waiting on some woman."

"You got that damn straight." Bryant didn't dare quench the thirst that had been hounding him since Ella showed up at his door.

Slouching down in the chair, he tipped his hat to the back of his head so he could keep an eye on the room. The regular waitress, Jolene, was working near the stage, laughing with the cowboys as she delivered beers to their tables. Her outfit, cheek-revealing denim shorts and a checkered blouse tied up to reveal her midriff, did little to flatter her figure.

He turned his head and nearly swallowed his tongue when he spotted Ella coming toward them. She was wearing the same damn outfit—Sal's idea of a waitress uniform. Only it looked a hell of a lot better on Ella. She had slender legs, her tanned thighs were firm and her stomach flat.

My God! What was she going to do when the baby began to show?

She gave him a Cheshire cat grin, her blue eyes gleaming behind her glasses. "What can I get you, gentlemen?"

"You can get the hell out of here," he said, his teeth—and other parts of his anatomy—clenching.

"I'll have a beer, sweetheart," Rusty said, giving her a thoroughly masculine once-over.

Bryant punched the man's arm. "Cool it!"

"Sure, boss." His foreman smothered a smile.

"Would you like a beer, too, cowboy?" she asked Bryant.

"I'm not a *cowboy,* Blondie. I'm—"

"I know exactly who you are, cowboy. The question now is, how well do you tip?" With a sexy twist of her hips, she turned and headed for the bar.

He saw red. He was so furious, he considered tossing her over his shoulder and taking her—

Where?

He didn't want to take her back to the ranch. He was better off with her gone sooner rather than later. Better off not exposing himself to the whims of a woman who could up and leave at the drop of a hat. She just hadn't gone far enough.

But for now, as he watched her make her way through the crowd, scooting past guys who ogled her in those revealing shorts, the operative answer to his question was that he wanted to take her to *bed.*

She brought them back two beers and set them on the table. "You want to run a tab?"

He caught her by the wrist, suddenly aware of how fragile her bones felt and how he outmatched her physically. "Rusty, take your beer and get lost. I need to talk to the lady."

Her cool gaze swept over Bryant like he was some kind of scuzzball. "Don't bother, Rusty. I've got work to do."

Rusty ignored Ella, hustling away from the table as if he'd been goosed by a bull with foot-long horns.

She lowered her gaze to where Bryant's big hand circled her wrist. "Let go of me."

"You can't be serious about working here. I've told you, I'll support you and the baby."

"An allowance. Very generous of you. I prefer to support myself."

"By being on your feet all day?"

"I'm only working two nights a week."

At least that was something. She wouldn't be mauled by the local talent every night of the week—only the busiest ones. "What about all this smoke? That can't be good for the baby."

She blinked as though he'd finally scored, then gave him a steely eyed look. "If you don't let go, I'm going to have to *make* you let go."

Somehow, despite her small size, he didn't doubt for a moment she'd do just that. He was learning Ella Papadakis had an iron will.

"Okay, Blondie." He released her. "But we're not done with this conversation yet."

"I am, unless you can come up with a more interesting topic." She left him to drink his beer alone and contemplate his next move.

ELLA DIDN'T DRAW a relaxed breath until the bar closed and Sal locked up. Bryant had watched her all night with those intense eyes of his, drinking steadily and never letting her out of his sight. Whenever a cowboy started acting up, Bryant had been right there, intimidating the man into behaving himself.

Though she bristled at his possessiveness, she felt oddly grateful for his protection. Not that she couldn't have handled a few cowboys. They didn't hold a candle to the muggers on Manhattan subways. Mostly, in a part of the country where men far outnumbered women, they just wanted to talk.

Bryant had also tried to insist he drive her home. She'd assured him that she was a lot more sober than he was and asked Rusty, who'd made two beers last the entire night, to be behind the wheel on the trip back to the ranch.

She smiled, though, at the tip Bryant had left her. A very generous man, it seemed. Or even drunker than she'd realized.

Behind the bar, Sal was counting out the cash receipts while Ella tried to sort her tips. Better than last night, she realized. And her feet and back were also twice as tired. Clearly, bookkeeping was more her calling than being a waitress.

"Saw you talking to Bryant tonight," Sal commented.

"Hmm." Sitting on a bar stool, Ella stretched, rolling her neck, feeling the weariness that ran clear down her spine to her toes.

"He doesn't come in much, not since he was a youngster."

She gave a noncommittal shrug.

"Stayed a long time, too," Sal added.

"Must have liked the music." Which was deafening. After two nights, Ella was sure her eardrums would never be the same again.

Sal leaned across the bar. "Just how long have you known Bryant?"

"Not long."

Obviously, Sal had a suspicious nature—or a very keen mind. Probably both. "Long enough for him to be crazy about you, would be my guess."

Heat flooded Ella's cheeks, but in the dim light she hoped her blush wouldn't be too obvious. "I think you've got that wrong."

"Nope." She shoved the cash register drawer closed. "That young fella may not know it yet, but he's got it bad for you. Hang in there, Ella P. Whatever you're doing, you're doing it jest right to snag yourself a good man."

"I don't think he wants to be snagged."

"None of them fellas on the soaps do, neither. Still, they don't have much choice when the girls put their minds to it, do they?"

Ella doubted that was the truth in her case. She'd tried to "snag" other men, or at least catch their attention. Evidently no one had given her the right script. In high school, Carlton Kavakian—the object of an awesome crush—had totally ignored her. In college, Stuart Smith had reacted the same way to her none-too-subtle flirtation. Not that she had been without *some* dates. She simply hadn't interested the men who appealed to her.

And Bryant was so much more than any of those men—boys—had been. She didn't think she had much of a chance to snag him. Not permanently.

But he had come to Sal's to seek her out tonight, she reminded herself. Perhaps, despite her limitations as a femme fatale, her plan was working. For the sake of her baby and her own good standing with her family, she hoped so.

HE HADN'T SLEPT worth a darn, the sun was coming up and now he had the grandmother of all hangovers. He wasn't used to drinking, not anymore. And the only way he was going to get his life back together again was to convince Ella to give it up, to go back to L.A. where she belonged. That way he wouldn't risk missing what he'd never had.

He parked his truck in front of the bungalow she'd rented. Moving gingerly so he wouldn't wake the gremlins in his head, he walked up the porch steps and knocked on the screen door.

She opened the door a crack, her hair sleep-mussed. She'd draped a lightweight robe over her shoulders, but he could still see her cotton nightgown and the dusky shadow of her nipples pressed against the fabric. Instinctively, his fingers flexed. He wanted his hands on her, wanted to feel the weight of her breasts in his palms.

"Do you have any idea what time it is?" she asked.

He swallowed hard; sweat dampened his forehead. "I had trouble sleeping."

"Maybe that has something to do with how much you drank last night."

"Possibly." But she'd also been the culprit. "Can I come in?"

Hesitating for a minute, she finally opened the door wider, stepped back and tied the robe more securely around her waist. "I can make you some coffee, if you'd like."

"I thought you didn't drink coffee."

"I bought some for company."

For company? Was she entertaining guests already? Some of those fool cowboys who'd been so eager to grab a handful of her last night?

He followed her through the living room and small dining room, neither of which contained a stick of furniture, then into the kitchen. At least she had a stove and refrigerator.

"How can you live in an empty house?"

"My furniture comes this week." She ran water into a saucepan. "The coffee's instant. Hope you don't mind. My coffeemaker is probably in Utah about now."

"You're really moving up here? Permanently?"

"Lock, stock and coffeemaker."

"But your job in L.A.—"

"I quit. Rolled what few retirement benefits I'd acquired into an IRA."

My God, she'd burned her bridges. "That might not have been too smart."

She glanced up at him. "I picked a mutual fund with a very good track record."

That wasn't what he'd meant. "You don't actually expect to earn a living working two nights a week at Sal's, do you? You won't even be able to make the rent on this matchbox."

She raised her eyebrows at his comment. "I *like* this house. And besides, I'm starting a bookkeeping service, too. I've already got one customer. If I can pick up a few more, I'll be in fat city."

The gremlins started hammering inside his skull again. She was determined to stay here and make his life crazy. "Where'd you learn to do bookkeeping?"

"New York University. At least, that's where I got my business degree. Magna cum laude," she added proudly. "All I'll need to do is get a book-keeping program for my computer, which hopefully arrives intact along with my coffeemaker."

A brain. He should have known. "I went to Montana State. Ag major. I hated accounting." And his grade point average wasn't anything to brag about.

"Most people do. That's why they hire someone else to keep their books." From a cupboard over the counter, she retrieved a cup and saucer, then spooned coffee into the cup. Two teaspoons.

This morning he probably needed three. In contrast, she looked too damn cheerful. Her cheeks glowed with good health, her lips were rosy without a trace of makeup. He wondered that he hadn't noticed how natural she looked, so chaste, when in fact he knew she was the sexiest woman he'd ever met. A virgin without an ounce of experience, she'd seduced him, aroused him beyond reason and given him the best night of lovemaking he'd ever had.

And he hadn't even known her name.

He did now, and still he wanted to pull her beneath him again, slip into her warmth, hear her startled cry turn to murmurs of pleasure.

"Did you plan to drink your coffee, or just stand there staring at me?"

He blinked, then looked at the cup in Ella's soft, delicate hands, and cleared his throat. He remembered just how those hands had felt smoothing over his chest, teasing ever closer to his arousal. "Thanks."

"Why don't you take it out to the porch and sit on the steps while I put some clothes on? There's really nowhere else to sit."

"Sure." Though he wished he'd been invited to help her take her clothes *off*.

As he settled onto the front steps, he realized if he went along with her idea of marriage, he'd have the right to do just that.

Except she'd only proposed the idea in order to get a name for her baby. To please her parents.

Maybe she hadn't intended that they sleep together again. Maybe she'd planned to be celibate.

Aw, hell! That would be torture.

The screen door creaked, and she stepped outside. "There, that's better. I'm not used to entertaining company in my nightgown."

"Glad to hear it," he said with a renewed case of morning-after grouchiness.

She sat down beside him, leaning back against the porch railing, and did that funny thing with her glasses, shoving them up on her nose with the tip of her finger when they slipped out of place. An unconscious mannerism, he suspected, and one she performed more often when she was nervous.

"I love it out here at sunset. The view is incredible."

The view wasn't that much different from the one at the Double S. "Have you told your folks yet? About the baby, I mean."

"Actually, no." She studied her fingernails, unadorned by any polish. "I...uh...guess I'll have to do that pretty soon."

"Did you know the owner of the local paper has been nosing around?"

"Winifred?" she asked.

He nodded.

"She showed up at Sal's on Friday asking questions. Guess any increase in the town's population is news."

"In addition to publishing the paper, she's the chief of the local morality police. She's capable of writing a lot of snide things about people in her paper, particularly if there's a hint of scandal involved."

"Well, I suspect at some point people will notice I'm pregnant and there's no daddy around. They'll question my morals, but they won't know—"

"There's nothing wrong with your morals," he said tautly.

"A lot of people, including my parents, might say otherwise."

"If you'd just go back to L.A.—"

"Sorry. I don't mean to be a burr under your saddle, Bryant, but I really like it here. This is where I want to raise our child."

Our child. Diane had used the same words—a lie that had cost him more than he had thought possible. In his heart, if not in fact, he'd been that baby's father. It had nearly killed him to lose that little girl, to have her and all the plans he'd made for her simply evaporate when her mother decided to take off.

Even more bitter to swallow was the realization that if there had been an unintended pregnancy for Ella, Cliff was meant to be the father. Bryant had been the one to cross the line.

When his twin had called last week to catch up on the news of home, Bryant had tried to casually bring up the subject of Ella. To admit what he'd done. But the words had stuck in his throat. She'd be gone from Montana soon enough. There was no reason to let Cliff know what a fool his big brother had been.

But if she stuck around…

Bryant tossed his unfinished coffee into the weed-infested flower bed and stood. "Like you said, you're over twenty-one. Do what you want."

FOR THE REST of the week Bryant was too busy to do much thinking, which was exactly how he liked it. The temperature had soared, the creeks dried up and the cattle had to be moved to where water was more plentiful. To no one's surprise, not all of the ancient equipment—the tractor and plows—was still functioning after a long winter. Parts had to be ordered, repairs made.

But by Friday night, Bryant had things back under control. And then he started thinking again.

About Ella.

Montana was a great place to live, but why would a city girl like Ella be so all-fired determined to stay? Being a single, unmarried mother in L.A. wouldn't hardly be out of the ordinary. So why hang around here where folks were sure to take note?

He paced the house—a place meant for a family, not a man alone. He'd tried to fill a bedroom once with a child but it turned out Terrilynn wasn't his to raise. She belonged to another man. So had Diane.

Ella didn't even appear to need his financial support. Hell, she'd started her own business! If the price of cattle kept dropping, she'd probably end up with more money in the bank than he had.

As the hour grew later, he started worrying about what was going on down at Sal's.

A woman like Ella shouldn't have to deal with rough-and-ready cowboys. She needed some protection.

This time he drove himself to town.

Sal's parking lot was filled with half-busted trucks and run-down old cars. Music—if that's what you called a heavy thump-thump of a base fiddle—

spilled past the swinging doors and into the street. The smell of cigarette smoke was evident from fifty feet, the smell of booze from a hundred.

Bryant shoved his way inside. Instantly the dense smoke caused his eyes to water. He swore under his breath. Damn it! This couldn't be good for Ella...or the baby. *His* baby, he thought furiously.

He spotted Ella, a tray under her arm, laughing with some of his own cowhands. He ground his teeth together. Next roundup, those two knuckle-brained cowpokes were going to be riding drag.

Striding across the room, ignoring anybody who was in his way, he reached Ella's side and took the tray from her, slamming it on the table.

"Okay, we'll do it your way." A muscle flexed in his jaw and his teeth hurt from grinding them.

Her head snapped up. Behind owlish glasses, her eyes opened wide. "What way is that?"

The two cowhands scooted their chairs out of the way. Turning toward the stage, they pretended to listen to the earsplitting music. Fortunately the combo was so loud, there was no way anyone could eavesdrop.

"We're going to get married. *Temporarily.*" He added plenty of emphasis so there would be no question what he had in mind—an idea that had bolted through him like lightning the moment he'd seen her chatting it up with his cowhands.

She hesitated, eyeing him skeptically. "What brought on this sudden change of heart?"

"Let's just say I don't like the idea of my kid

inhaling a carton's worth of cigarette smoke every night.''

"I see.'' She swallowed visibly and licked her lips. ''How soon are you thinking—''

"There's a three-day waiting period. Considering it's the weekend, I figure by Wednesday, or Thursday at the latest, we ought to have our ducks in a row.''

"You said temporarily—''

"That's what you wanted, isn't it? A name to give your baby.'' He leaned very close to her. ''So here's the deal. You get the name you're after, your record as a Goody Two-shoes stays clean as a whistle and you keep your folks happy.''

"Hey, Ella-baby,'' a man shouted from a neighboring table. ''How 'bout a round over here?''

With a tight smile, she waved an acknowledgment.

Bryant cringed. *Ella-baby!* He ought to knock some sense into the guy's—

"What do you get in return?'' Ella asked, focusing again on Bryant.

Not nearly as much as he wanted. ''A clear conscience and a kid who doesn't grow up labeled illegitimate.'' And maybe with a decent lawyer, he'd even get visitation rights. Eventually.

She gazed at him steadily. ''You're talking about a marriage in name only. A temporary arrangement until the baby arrives.''

"That's the deal. Take it or leave it.''

The music came to a sudden halt, the cowpokes strangely quiet. It was like a freeze frame on TV or the earth spinning to a stop. Bryant's heart seized as he waited for her answer. He wasn't going to get himself messed up like he had with Diane. This time both he and his *wife* would know where they stood.

"I'll take it," she whispered. *"Temporarily."*

He wasn't sure he liked her tone or the stubborn lift of her chin. Damn it all! She was up to something. But the relief that surged through him eased the band that had been tightening around his chest. His shoulders relaxed. God, he hoped he wasn't making the worst mistake of his life.

"Okay, get your things," he said. "I'll take you back to the ranch with me."

"Can you hurry it up?" shouted the guy at the next table. "We ain't got all day, ya know."

She gave the customer another wave and a weak smile. "I can't leave in the middle of my shift," she told Bryant. "What would Sal do?"

"The hell with Sal. She'll get by." He took Ella by the arm.

"Oh, no you don't, cowboy." She shrugged out of his grasp. "I agreed to marry you—temporarily—but that doesn't give you the right to manhandle me."

"I'm not man—"

"Nor does it give you the right to tell me where I can work or for how long. If you want a trained poodle on a leash for a wife, try somebody else."

His nerves as taut as a kite string, his need was about to tear him apart. He didn't like the way things were going and he didn't want a poodle. He wanted Ella in his bed, but he wasn't going to take her there. The price he'd pay was too high. She was the most mule-headed woman he'd ever had the misfortune to meet. And he was getting damn frustrated about the entire marital scheme.

"If you insist on risking death by smoke inhalation, then I'll wait for you till closing."

"That's really not necessary." Picking up the tray, she headed toward the bar.

He blocked her way. "I want you at the ranch."

She glanced around to see that no one was paying any attention to them, the audience back to listening to the blaring music. "Why? So I can make your breakfast for you?"

"I can make my own damn breakfast. I've been doing it for years."

"Then a few more days won't hurt you." She tried to sidestep away but there was no room to maneuver among the crowded tables.

His gaze skimmed across her breasts and slid down to her flat belly. "Let's just say I want to protect my investment."

Ella drew in a sharp, pungent breath of smoky air, intensely aware of the way he was looking at her. He'd just proposed to her and was thinking about sex. Hot, sweaty-body sex. Certainly there was no element of love in his offer, or apparent in his eyes. But, despite the potent lust she saw, he didn't intend that they ever make love again.

Her determination faltered. How could she possibly agree to marry a man who made no pretense of loving her?

But in the next instant, she knew she couldn't do anything else. This was what she wanted. What she'd asked for. A marriage license so she wouldn't disgrace her family.

Meanwhile, call it fate, karma, dumb luck or an added bonus, she was stuck on Bryant Swain. There was enough chemistry between them to ignite a wildfire, and it wasn't all on her side of the equation if she could go by his heated look.

"Let's plan on a Thursday wedding," she suggested, her head still reeling that she'd actually agreed to a marriage in name only. This virtual stranger was the man she'd see at breakfast every morning for the next six and a half months. Or longer, if she had her way. "I'll call my folks to invite them."

A scowl angled his ginger-brown eyebrows downward. "Let's not make too big a deal of this."

"It could well be the only wedding I'll ever have. Real or not, I want them to be here."

Chapter Eight

Ella heard the car when it pulled into her driveway and she rushed outside to welcome her family. Melissa was the first to burst out of the rental vehicle, all energy and flying blond pigtails.

"Aunt Ella!" The six-year-old raced up the walkway and Ella scooped her up in her arms. "Mommy says I get to be your flower girl. Do I?"

Ella planted a kiss on the top of the child's head. "You certainly do. I wouldn't think of getting married without you as my flower girl."

Melissa beamed. "What kind of flowers do I get to carry?"

"Oh, all kinds. Montana wildflowers." She'd ordered them from a florist in Great Falls to be delivered to the church tomorrow before the ceremony. A bouquet for herself and a smaller one for Melissa, all in the effort to make this appear to be a "real" wedding.

"Cool," her niece said.

Ella eased Melissa to the ground so she could hug her mother and father.

"This is so exciting, dear," her mother said. She smelled of lilacs and her dress was slightly wrinkled from the long flight. "But it's all so sudden, you getting married, and here in Montana, for heaven's sake. You just moved here! Are you sure—"

"I had to pay through the nose for our airline tickets," her father grumbled. "Hardly worth the expense when we're going back home tomorrow. Not that I can be away from the store any longer than that, but I don't know what all the rush is about."

"Remember you're getting off cheap when it comes to the wedding, Papa. No fancy gown or sit-down dinner for me." Ella kissed him on the cheek. "So, how was your trip?"

"Fine till we got to town," he said, still in a complaining mood. He shoved his fingers through his already-mussed silver-gray hair. "Some ancient Buick got in front of me and the old duffer driving it couldn't get that clunker to go faster than ten miles an hour."

"Your father started to swear like a sailor," Margaret said, feigning shock. "And our windows were open. No telling what all your neighbors are thinking about us."

Ella laughed. "That had to be Mr. O'Reilly in the Buick. His grandfather was the town founder. I met him once at the grocery store. He's a sweet man and seems kind of lonely."

"Can't drive worth a damn."

That from a man who'd never owned a car and

had probably driven a total of ten times in his entire life, and then only on vacations.

She reached out to embrace her sister, whose expression was almost as strained as Papa's. Every inch a sophisticated New Yorker, she wore a tailored salmon suit with a skirt that reached only to midthigh. Not a hair on her head was out of place, no wrinkles dared show themselves. And when Tasha walked, she seemed to float on a cushion of air, just the way she strolled so elegantly down a runway showing off the latest designs.

"I'm so glad you came, Tasha, and brought Melissa, too."

"Hey, what's a sister for?"

Still grumbling, Papa said, "At least Tasha isn't rushing to the altar this time. Weddings shouldn't be hurried."

Ignoring her father, Ella said, "I thought maybe Nick would come along, too."

Tasha's gaze slid toward the house with its inviting porch. "He's real busy at the office. New clients and all."

"You haven't set a date yet?"

"Not exactly. He has me lined up to show the fall fashions in Paris, which he thinks will be quite a feather in my cap."

"Hmm, you could have a honeymoon in Paris. That would be nice."

Tasha shrugged. "You know Nick. Being an agent comes first. He doesn't like to mix business with pleasure."

Ella suspected Tasha's agent-fiancé was more interested in his percent of her income than in establishing a family. "So, when will you get married?"

"We're still thinking next spring for the wedding."

That would be after Ella's baby was due. At least she wouldn't have to wear a maternity gown for the ceremony.

Their mother spoke up. "I don't know why Tasha's putting it off so long. Nick's such a nice man, and he's rich, too. I say, let's get on with the wedding."

"Money isn't everything, Mama," Tasha said.

Sensing something wasn't quite right with her sister's wedding plans, Ella hooked her arm through Tasha's. She and Tasha would have time to talk later that evening. "Let's get your bags inside. I've got dinner practically ready."

"Where's your young man, dear?" Ella's mother asked. "I thought he might be here to greet us."

It was Ella's turn not to meet her mother's gaze. "He's like Nick, I guess. He's got a lot of work to do." She'd invited him to come to dinner tonight when they'd gotten their marriage license. He'd declined and, on his own, he'd decided they shouldn't see much of each other until the wedding. In some ways she was relieved. The strain of being around him and knowing their marriage would be a sham was a reality she'd just as soon ignore.

In other ways she regretted his decision. They were still virtual strangers. They could have used the time to get better acquainted. Her foolish heart kept hoping he'd change his mind, that their marriage would be more than pretend.

The net result, however, was that Ella had been suffering from a bad case of insomnia, despite her pregnancy.

How on earth could her sister handle a long engagement? For Ella, the past five days had been an eternity. And yet, in the blink of an eye, her wedding day would arrive. As far as the world would know, she'd be Mrs. Bryant Swain, safely married before she had to announce her pregnancy.

But she wouldn't be his wife, not in any meaningful way.

AFTER DINNER, Papa complained of the time change. Her mother was tired, too, so they both retired to the master bedroom, making their way around the boxes that Ella hadn't bothered to unpack since the movers delivered them. She'd just have to do it all over again at the ranch.

Melissa was still excited about the trip and the wedding tomorrow, but eventually Tasha coaxed her daughter into going to bed. That left Ella and Tasha to visit by themselves.

"Why are you putting off your wedding date?" Ella asked before her sister had a chance to question her own hasty marriage. Their legs curled under them, they'd settled at either end of the couch where Ella would sleep her last night as a single woman.

Tasha pulled the pillow in front of her and hugged it. "I guess I'm still reeling from the fiasco

How To Play:

No Risk !

1. With a coin, carefully scratch off the 3 gold areas on your Lucky Carnival Wheel. By doing so you have qualified to receive everything revealed — 2 FREE books and a surprise gift — ABSOLUTELY FREE!

2. Send back this card and you'll receive brand-new Harlequin American Romance® novels. These books have a cover price of $4.25 each in the U.S. and $4.99 each in Canada, but they are yours TOTALLY FREE!

3. There's no catch! You're under no obligation to buy anything. We charge nothing — ZERO — for your first shipment. And you don't have to make any minimum number of purchases — not even one!

4. The fact is thousands of readers enjoy receiving books by mail from the Harlequin Reader Service®. They enjoy the convenience of home delivery...they like getting the best new novels at discount prices, BEFORE they're available in stores...and they love their *Heart to Heart* subscriber newsletter featuring author news, horoscopes, recipes, book reviews and much more!

5. We hope that after receiving your free books you'll want to remain a subscriber. But the choice is yours — to continue or cancel, anytime at all! So why not take us up on our invitation, with no risk of any kind. You'll be glad you did.

No Cost!

LUCKY

Find Out Instantly The Gifts You Get
Absolutely FREE!

Carnival Wheel

Scratch-off Game →

Scratch off
ALL 3
Gold areas

YES!

I have scratched off the 3 Gold Areas above.
Please send me the 2 FREE books and gift for
which I qualify! I understand I am under no
obligation to purchase any books, as explained on the back and
on the opposite page.

354 HDL CY42   **154 HDL CY4S**

NAME   (PLEASE PRINT CLEARLY)

ADDRESS

APT.#   CITY

STATE/PROV.   ZIP/POSTAL CODE

Offer limited to one per household and not valid to current   **(H-AR-05/00)**
Harlequin American Romance® subscribers. All orders subject to approval.

The Harlequin Reader Service® — Here's how it works:

Accepting your 2 free books and gift places you under no obligation to buy anything. You may keep the books and gift and return the shipping statement marked "cancel." If you do not cancel, about a month later we'll send you 4 additional novels and bill you just $3.57 each in the U.S., or $3.96 each in Canada, plus 25¢ delivery per book and applicable taxes if any. * That's the complete price and — compared to cover prices of $4.25 each in the U.S. and $4.99 each in Canada — it's quite a bargain! You may cancel at any time, but if you choose to continue, every month we'll send you 4 more books, which you may either purchase at the discount price or return to us and cancel your subscription.

*Terms and prices subject to change without notice. Sales tax applicable in N.Y. Canadian residents will be charged applicable provincial taxes and GST.

If offer card is missing write to: Harlequin Reader Service, 3010 Walden Ave., P.O. Box 1867, Buffalo, NY 14240-1867

BUSINESS REPLY MAIL
FIRST-CLASS MAIL   PERMIT NO. 717   BUFFALO, NY

POSTAGE WILL BE PAID BY ADDRESSEE

HARLEQUIN READER SERVICE
3010 WALDEN AVE
PO BOX 1867
BUFFALO NY 14240-9952

NO POSTAGE
NECESSARY
IF MAILED
IN THE
UNITED STATES

of my first marriage. I don't want to make the same mistake again.''

''I kind of assumed you were in love with Nick, since you accepted his ring. Have you changed your mind?''

Glancing at the nearly five-karat ring she wore, Tasha tightened her fingers into a fist. ''How does anyone know whether it's really love, or simply good timing and the course of least resistance?''

Ella wasn't sure she could answer that question, certainly not for another person. What she felt for Bryant was too volatile for a simple definition.

Eyeing her suspiciously, Tasha asked, ''You do love this cowboy you're about to marry, don't you?''

Keeping her gaze steady, she said, ''I wouldn't marry a man unless I loved him.''

''He must be some kind of cowboy to have this happen so fast. You've always been coolheaded, Ella—Daddy's sweet little angel. I sure hope he feels the same way about you.''

''Not yet,'' Ella conceded. ''But I've always thrived on a challenge.''

Tasha's expression clouded. ''Then he's not the reason this wedding is happening so suddenly?''

''He's the reason, all right.'' Ella took a deep breath, knowing she couldn't keep her secret much longer. ''I'm pregnant.''

''Oh, Sis, I don't know what to—''

''Don't tell the folks, okay? I know they'll figure it out soon enough on their own, but they are so traditional. I don't want to hurt them.''

"I won't breathe a word...but, Ella, you were always so...so—"

"Prissy. I know." She lifted her shoulders in a self-deprecating shrug. "Looks like getting pregnant at the drop of a hat runs in our family."

Tasha paled. Obviously unable to come up with an easy quip, she scooted to Ella's end of the couch and gave her a hug.

"Thanks for being here, Sis," Ella said. "I appreciate it."

"You were there for me when I needed you. I'm just returning the favor."

THEY GOT TO the church in Reilly's Gulch precisely at ten the next morning, per Bryant's instructions. He and Rusty were waiting for them out front, Bryant dressed in a dark citified suit and a somber tie. Though strikingly handsome, he looked more *GQ* than *Cowboy Monthly*. Ella decided she preferred the cowboy edition—including hip-hugging jeans.

Introductions were a bit awkward, particularly since her father was still in a grumpy mood. He hated to be away from his menswear store, the place where Ella had learned her early lessons in retailing.

To her surprise, there was no sign of Cliff. She'd thought sure Bryant would invite his twin to the wedding, and she'd been anxious about their first meeting since the *incident.*

"I need to see you for a minute," Bryant said to her. "In the preacher's office."

Her nerves tangling together, she excused herself,

leaving her family in Rusty's care as he provided them with the digest version of the history of Reilly's Gulch. Surely Bryant wasn't going to call off the wedding at this late date.

Gripping her arm firmly, he whisked her into the church office. Bookcases filled to overflowing lined the room. The desk was equally cluttered except for a cleared space in the middle where a legal-looking document had been placed.

"There are some papers I need you to sign," he said. His aftershave had a light, spicy scent that didn't quite smother the lingering aroma of cowboy leather and hard work.

"Papers? We've already got the license."

He handed her the document. "It's a prenuptial agreement. Cliff and I own the Double S together. I can't put his half at risk, and I don't want to jeopardize my interests, either. These papers will make sure you and I both come out of the marriage with exactly what we have going into it."

That sounded reasonable to Ella. In fact, since Bryant was obviously planning for an early demise to their sham marriage, she'd be smart to protect her own assets, as limited as they might be. She would, after all, have a child to support if marital bliss eluded her.

Taking the papers from him, she began to scan the legalese. It all seemed quite reasonable until she came to the section on child custody.

Her head snapped up. "I'm not going to give up custody of my baby."

"You claim the baby is mine, so I've got some

rights, too. I won't have you taking my kid off to L.A. or New York and leaving me high and dry. I went that route with Diane. If you leave the county, then I want—''

''I'm not planning to go anywhere, Bryant. I'm staying right here. And don't confuse me with Diane. I've never lied to you and I believe a baby needs both a mother and a father. *If* we get a divorce—''

''When—''

''We'll negotiate visitation rights then. But no way am I going to give you full custody of my baby.''

His expressive eyebrows lowered into a frown. ''If that's the way you feel, maybe we'd better cancel the wedding.''

Afraid she was about to risk everything by taking a firm stand, she swallowed hard. ''You can't blackmail me into signing that agreement if it means losing custody of my baby. And when you think about it, I don't imagine you'd want a wife who'd cave in so easily about something that important.''

Bryant glared at her. There weren't many people who'd stand up to him the way Ella did. That she was fiercely protective of her unborn child was oddly reassuring. Still, it didn't mean he'd easily give up his own kid if Ella decided to take off with the baby.

Mothers held all the cards in a custody suit, his attorney had told him.

Hell! He didn't have a chance in Hades of win-

ning the battle anyway, prenuptial or not. The cards
were stacked against him. They always had been,
reading loud and clear that he didn't deserve a family.

He snatched the document from Ella, flattened it
on the desktop and used one of the preacher's pens
to cross out the useless clause, initialing the change.
"All right, we'll settle that dispute when the time
comes." He offered her the pen. "You got any
more problems with the agreement?"

She shook her head, her eyes surprisingly bright
as she took the pen and signed her name in a flowing feminine script.

At least he'd protected his ranch, he thought. But
not his child. And maybe not himself.

He turned to leave, but Ella stopped him.

"Wasn't Cliff able to get away from L.A. for the
wedding?" she asked. "I thought for sure he'd be
here."

His stomach knotted. "Since this whole marriage
is only temporary, I didn't want to trouble him."

"I see." Her chin trembled slightly and she
glanced away. "I know you're only going through
with this for the sake of the baby, but could you
make it look real? So my parents won't..." Her
voice caught.

He almost pulled her into his arms to reassure
her that everything would be all right. But he was
afraid to believe that himself. "Don't worry," he
said instead. "I'll put on a good show."

WHEN BRYANT ANNOUNCED he and his bride-to-be
had completed their business, Preacher Goodfellow

led them into the church, where the whole wedding party stood in front of the altar. Between his white hair, which he'd combed into wings next to his ears, and his white gown, the preacher resembled an aging angel. He began the service with a sermon more suitable for a revivalist tent than a wedding ceremony.

Distracted by the tears Mrs. Papadakis seemed determined to shed and Ella's sweet wildflower scent, Bryant wasn't particularly aware of the vows when the preacher got to that part of the service.

He had the uncanny feeling this marriage wasn't going to work out as he expected. Keeping his vow not to bed Ella was going to be like impaling himself on his own stupidity. But he had to keep an emotional distance from her and he couldn't do that if he let himself forget the truth.

Sure as the sun comes up in the morning, she'd leave him for greener pastures. Or in her case, more asphalt pavement.

No way she'd last through a Montana winter. She was too fragile. Too vulnerable for a part of the country where it took guts to simply survive.

She was wearing a pastel-blue dress made of silk that clung to her breasts and flowed over her hips. A city dress. Not one a woman would have use for on a ranch where there wouldn't be anyone to notice the contrast between the subdued color of her dress and the vibrant cornflower-blue of her eyes.

And her hands were too soft for the hard work a rancher's wife had to do, he thought as he slipped a plain gold band on her finger. Her neatly polished fingernails would be broken within days, jagged reminders of the life she'd given up.

He gritted his teeth. When she left him, she'd take the child he hadn't intended to sire with her.

To his surprise, Ella produced a ring for him, too. A gold band much like the one she now wore, symbols of the promises neither of them intended to keep.

He steeled himself for the end of the ceremony. He was under control now. He didn't want to lose his composure in a kiss like the ones he'd been dreaming about all week. This wedding was make-believe. There would be none of the deep, hungry kisses he longed for, not if he was going to survive the next few months.

"You may kiss the bride," the preacher said.

Turning, Bryant lowered his head toward Ella. For a moment, he locked his gaze on her brilliant blue eyes. The world shifted around him; his equilibrium teetered on the edge between apprehension and anticipation. *His wife. The mother of his child.*

Closing his eyes to the dizzying reality of what he'd just done, he brushed a kiss to her delicately sculpted lips, promising himself he'd only take that one taste. Anything more and he'd be addicted to her flavor.

When he lifted his head, Ella let a sigh escape. All morning she'd been anticipating this moment, the sealing of their wedding vows. With the feel of his lips on hers, all the tactile memories of their night together came racing back, warming her with remembered pleasure. This felt so *right,* being Bryant's wife. In his eyes she saw the restraint his simple kiss had cost him…and his desire. Despite the unconventional circumstances of their marriage, she celebrated the baby and the vows that now bound them together—for a while.

Somehow she had to keep her hopes alive for their future.

She'd barely taken a steadying breath when Rusty stepped forward.

"Mind if an old goat like me claims a chance to kiss the bride?" he asked, grinning.

"My pleasure, Rusty."

"Don't enjoy it too much," Bryant grumbled, and Ella wasn't sure if he was making the remark for her benefit or Rusty's.

Within moments her father claimed a kiss, too, and she hugged her mother and sister.

"You're absolutely glowing, Sis," Tasha said. "Too bad there's no one here to take your picture."

Right on cue, the back door to the church swung open and in marched Winifred Bruhn, notepad in hand and a camera dangling around her neck.

"I'm supposed to be told when there's going to be a wedding," she complained. "How the devil do you expect me to report the news if no one keeps the press informed?"

"Maybe we're keeping it a secret," Bryant said.

"Hogwash." She raised her camera to her eye. "Git on over there next to your bride, Bryant. And for lord's sake, try not to look so grumpy."

With little enthusiasm, he stepped beside Ella,

slipping his arm around her waist. The flash went off, blinding Ella.

''Now then, let's get a shot of the bride tossing her bouquet.'' Winifred motioned the group to re-form as if she were a Hollywood movie producer. ''Where are all the single women?''

''I'm it,'' Tasha admitted, raising her hand.

''I'm single, too,'' Melissa protested. ''Can't I catch the bouquet?''

Everyone laughed except Papa, and Winifred organized the bouquet toss with Tasha and her daughter in competition with each other. Fortunately Tasha's arms were longer. She reeled in the prize.

Melissa pouted. ''You should have thrown it to me, Aunt Ella.''

Kneeling beside her niece, Ella said, ''Honey, you'll have lots of chances to catch a bridal bouquet. And you don't want your mother to have to wait until you're all grown up before she marries Nick, do you?''

Melissa hung her head, and Ella noticed tears in her eyes.

''I don't want Mama to marry Nick,'' she whispered, her chin trembling. ''He doesn't like me.''

Worried that the child's attitude might not bode well for the next wedding in the family, Ella shot a worried glance at her sister. Suddenly Ella wished she had more time to talk with Tasha, but the editor of the *Reed County Register* was too busy choreographing the wedding party's photograph album.

That task completed, they moved into the church's social hall. The minister's wife had prepared tea sandwiches for them, punch and cookies, insisting there had to be a reception where everyone could celebrate the joyous occasion.

Scratching his curly fringe of red hair, Rusty said, "Reckon a reception at Sal's would be a helluva lot more fun."

Suppressing a giggle, Ella elbowed him in the ribs. "Hush. Arranging all of this was very thoughtful of Mrs. Goodfellow."

"Bryant don't look like he's having a real good time."

No, he didn't, she had to concede. Her father had button-holed Bryant in a corner of the room, no doubt giving him the third degree in the same way he used to interrogate what few adolescent dates she'd had who showed up at the front door.

Finally her father announced they had to leave in order to catch their flight. Feeling guilty that she was glad to see them go, she said her goodbyes in the church parking lot with Bryant at her side.

As their car drove away, she said, "Whew. I guess my father gave you a real grilling, huh?"

"Not any more so than I'd do under the same circumstances if you were my daughter."

Amazed and pleased by his response, she looked up at him. "I think you're going to be a very good father."

He clamped his Stetson firmly on his head. "Come on, Mrs. Swain, let's get back to the ranch. Some of us have work to do."

The touch of sarcasm in his voice lessened the joy of hearing him use her new name, but it didn't alter the fact that she was, in the eyes of God and her parents, a married woman—who in a few weeks would have to announce she was pregnant.

SHE RODE IN Bryant's truck out to the ranch while Rusty drove her car. The ride was so silent, the tension between she and Bryant as palpable as the electricity before a lightning storm, that the big house was a welcome sight. *Her new home,* she mentally corrected, albeit one that Bryant considered would be only her temporary residence.

She felt a smile climb up from deep inside her. Though not a beauty like her sister, tenacity and determination had always been among Ella's finest attributes. Bryant Swain was about to learn that the hard way.

He parked the truck near the house and she climbed out. She squinted into the afternoon sun, scanning the rolling countryside with a proprietary eye. Someday all of this would be her child's legacy, she thought with pride, her hand instinctively palming her belly. No wonder Bryant didn't want to risk losing a square foot of his land. Neither did she.

"Welcome back to the Double S, missus."

She smiled at Bryant's aging foreman, who had parked her car behind the truck. "I'm glad to be here, Rusty."

"Reckon the boss's disposition will lighten up some now, you being where he can keep a close eye on you, 'n' all."

She chuckled. "I don't expect to be kept a prisoner, but I won't wander far from home, I can tell you that.''

''Yes, ma'am.'' He tipped his hat back on his forehead. ''Let me help you with your bags.''

''I'll get 'em, Rusty.'' Striding past them, Bryant popped the trunk open. ''After I get Ella settled, I'll come help you with the broken corral fence. Tomorrow we've got to haul whatever she won't be needing from her house in town to storage down in Great Falls.''

Ella said, ''We could sell most of the furniture—''

Bryant shot her a sharp look. ''I think it'd be a lot smarter if you hang on to it.'' His unspoken reminder ''You'll need furniture after the divorce'' lingered in the air between them.

Rusty gave her a curious look, and Ella glanced away, her high hopes faltering. Bryant was just as determined *not* to give their marriage a chance as she was to make it last. She was in for a battle of wills, and he held the ultimate power in his hands. At any minute, he could call it quits. She'd be left holding, literally, a baby…and, if she wasn't very careful, a broken heart.

He carried her luggage upstairs to the guest bedroom where she had stayed before, an exclamation point to the fact she was not Mrs. Swain in the eyes of her husband. More like an inconvenient boarder, she thought, fighting a sense of despair.

Perhaps she'd read him entirely wrong. Perhaps he didn't desire her at all. She wasn't sexy enough, or pretty enough, to measure up to a woman he'd willingly choose for a wife. It was only the baby who concerned him. After all, once before he'd agreed to a loveless marriage for the sake of a child. This situation was no different.

He dropped the two suitcases on the bed. "There's plenty of space in the closet for your clothes."

"Yes, I know. This should be fine." Her business suits wouldn't even need unpacking and were still in the boxes she'd bring over later from her house in town.

"I've got to change and get out to help Rusty and the boys."

"Of course."

He studied her as he undid his tie, tugging it from around his neck. "You okay with fixing dinner? There's plenty of meat in the freezer. Pick whatever you want."

"What time would you like to eat?"

"Like before. Whenever it gets dark, we eat. On a ranch there's work to be done as long as there's light. Sometimes longer."

Self-consciously, she licked her lips, aware of the bed she stood beside and how much she wished he'd make love to her there. "I'll have something ready for you."

He turned, started to leave the room.

"I haven't thanked you for, uh, saving my reputation with my folks," she said, unwilling for him to go so soon, to resume his life as if nothing had happened between them. Like a marriage.

"I didn't marry you because of your folks."

She held her breath, hoping beyond reason that he had another reason—one that involved love.

"I did it for the baby. I want to be damn sure my kid is a Swain."

She couldn't speak. Of all the foolish dreams she'd had, this one took the cake. That familiar realization lodged painfully in her throat and pressed tears to the backs of her eyes.

Not wanting him to see her cry, she said a choked out, "Excuse me," and fled into the bathroom down the hall, closing the door behind her. She yanked off her glasses and swiped at her tears with the back of her hand. Darn him! This was supposed to be her honeymoon—a nine-letter word signifying *whoopee!*

Chapter Nine

Bryant shoved his chair back from the kitchen table. He'd showered when he came in to dinner and his hair was still slightly damp, dark blond strands curling at his nape.

Mollie, who'd been curled up on the floor next to him, moved about three feet out of his way and settled down again.

"I've got some paperwork to do and then I plan to hit the sack," Bryant said.

Ella picked up his dirty plate and stacked it with hers. So much for her first night of marital bliss. "Bookkeeping?"

"Yeah, there's always bills to be paid."

"If you want me to, I'll set up a bookkeeping system for you like I'm planning to do for Sal."

He slanted her a speculative look. "I think I'd better stick with my shoe box system. Then when you leave, I'll still be able to figure out where I stand financially."

His words stung more sharply than if he had

slapped her. He was so *damn* determined to see their marriage fail.

She snatched the plates from the table and carried them to the sink, equally determined not to give up so easily. And not to let him see how much she wanted a real wedding night.

As a little girl, she'd dreamed of having a husband and children, living in a big house with a huge backyard—a yard big enough to have a horse. When she'd hit adolescence and found herself sitting home dateless more often than not on Saturday nights, she dreamed of a white knight arriving on his trusty steed, kissing her lightly and awakening the beautiful princess who'd been hiding behind her ugly glasses.

Well, she'd gotten the big backyard and then some. Thus far, the white knight had eluded her. But she didn't plan to give up her dreams just yet.

She covered the leftover chicken and rice with plastic wrap and put it in the refrigerator, then put the frying pan in the sink to soak. Her future was at stake and so was her baby's.

"Trust me, Mollie," she said to the dog. "This man never met stubborn until he met me."

The dog sank to the floor again, resting her chin on her paws, and blinked up at Ella with big brown, disbelieving eyes.

"All right, so I'm not the sexiest woman in the world. But I'm going to use whatever weapons I've got." As limited as they might be.

Upstairs she changed into her nightgown and a summer-weight robe, a modest combination but not entirely opaque in the right light. She wished she'd spent the past week dieting to lose the extra five or ten pounds she'd put on since college. Her thighs were too thick, her waist not nearly narrow enough and her breasts not anything to write home about. Living with her size-six sister, she knew exactly what a beautiful figure should look like.

Ella didn't have one.

But it was too late now. The die was cast.

Her mouth was dry as toast and her knees wobbly as she walked brazenly into Bryant's den where he was working at a big oak desk.

"Hi. I hope you don't mind me borrowing one of your books. I seem to be out of reading material."

His head came up; his eyes narrowed. "Help yourself."

"Thanks." She brushed past him, as close as she dared, and pretended to study the books that were stacked haphazardly in the bookcase behind his desk. She recalled from her original stay at his house that Bryant's literary tastes ranged from adventure and mystery novels to cattle management handbooks. It didn't matter which book she picked. What *did* matter was that she could feel his eyes on her, appraising her.

"Isn't it a bit late to start a book tonight?" he asked.

"I'm a little keyed up. I thought reading would help put me to sleep. Wedding-night jitters, I suppose." She managed a light laugh.

"Right."

She picked a book at random, started to leave the room, then stopped right beside his desk, glancing at the ledger he was working on. She was standing so close to him, she was sure he could detect the scent of her cologne, the tiny drops she'd applied behind her ears and knees while she was upstairs.

"You really should let me computerize all that before I leave," she said, her fingertips brushing the page. "It would make your life so much easier."

He cleared his throat. "I'll keep your offer in mind."

Nervously, she weighed the book in her hand. He wasn't going to fall for the bait she'd trolled past him. No doubt he was a hard man to hook or some other woman would have landed him by now. She'd have to rely on persistence—like a Chinese water torture—to wear him down.

"Well, I'd better get up to bed," she said. "I'll see you in the morning."

"Enjoy your reading."

"I will. Thanks."

Bryant didn't move until he heard Ella close the door to her room upstairs. He couldn't have, not without risking serious damage to an important part of his anatomy. As it was, the snaps on his jeans had come close to bursting. If he hadn't been sitting at his desk, she would have gotten a fair idea of how much her little show had affected him.

He remembered all too painfully when she'd fled to the bathroom earlier and he'd walked to his room. The massive bed there had mocked him. His wedding day, and he'd be sleeping alone.

He'd shed his wedding outfit, grabbed a work shirt from the closet and pulled it on. He'd needed hard labor to stay under control. But he'd known then it was going to be harder than riding a wild stallion.

And ride was exactly what he wanted to do with Ella—long and hard and fast. Unfortunately, that wasn't a choice he could permit himself.

And unfortunately it looked as if she wanted to change the rules of the game—to make their marriage more than in name only.

He couldn't afford to do that. Not if he expected to survive when she left him.

Leaning back in his swivel chair, he stacked his hands behind his head and gazed up at the ceiling, listening to the sounds of her moving around in her bedroom. Her figure, silhouetted beneath her gown, was all he remembered it to be. Shapely hips. Full breasts with just the hint of dusky rose nipples.

Some men liked their women downright skinny. He liked women with a little meat on their bones.

He chuckled a low, rough sound. He wondered who she thought she was fooling with her little stunt. The book she'd borrowed was *Breeding and Castrating Range Cattle.*

The hell of it was, *she* was the one who was breeding, and *he* was going to spend the next several months as frustrated as a castrated bull.

ELLA COULD LEARN to hate Bryant's alarm.

She'd been married a week and the darn thing

had startled her awake every morning even though her room was across the hall. None of those nice little clock chimes she was used to, or even a friendly disc jockey filled with early-morning good spirits to wake her.

No, Bryant had to have an alarm as shrill as a fire bell.

Perversely it didn't seem to bother Bryant at all. Or at least it took him forever to get the thing turned off every morning.

With a groan, she rolled out of bed, the morning air chill after the warmth of a down quilt.

She parted the curtains to get her morning fix of Montana. Definitely God's country. The first rays of sunrise had caught the upper branches of the cottonwood trees down by the creek, turning the leaves to a vibrant green against a sky painted pale blue and streaked with rose. She smiled. The view was worth at least two cups of coffee as a wake-me-up.

Dressing quickly, she brushed her hair and went downstairs to prepare breakfast. Fortunately her morning sickness was a thing of the past and the smell of food no longer bothered her early in the day. In fact, with all the fresh air she'd been getting, her appetite was more than healthy.

When Bryant arrived in the kitchen, he consumed his first cup of coffee and six pancakes before he spoke.

"What are your plans for today?" he asked.

She poured four more circles of pancake batter on the griddle. "I've got a doctor's appointment in

Great Falls, and then I'll do some grocery shopping in town.''

Standing, he walked to the counter where he poured himself another cup of coffee. ''Is something wrong?''

''No, just a routine appointment.''

''If you'd told me, I would have gone with you.''

''No need. I'm perfectly capable of driving that far and getting home in one piece again.''

He didn't look convinced. ''I'll tell Rusty to take one of the other hands to move the herd in the south pasture. I'll come with—''

''Bryant, that isn't necessary.'' She flipped the pancakes. ''While I'm in town, I'm going to shop for some maternity clothes. You'd be bored to death.''

His gaze slid to her midsection, taking in the loosely fitting blouse that masked the shape of her tummy. ''You need them already?''

''I haven't been able to snap my jeans for a week, and I suspect it's not simply because I'm eating more calories than usual.'' Though feeding a cowboy involved a lot more food than she had realized, between her appetite and his hunger, there weren't many leftovers. ''I figured as long as I was going to be in Great Falls anyway, I'd do some shopping. The dry goods store in Reilly's Gulch doesn't have a big selection of maternity clothes.''

''I still think I should—''

''No. You have your own work to do. I'd rather go alone.'' In fact, after a week on the ranch, she was ready to be off by herself. She and Bryant had been traveling a tight rope, the sexual tension between them as sharp as a razor edge. He wasn't about to give in to it and she couldn't force him. She needed a breather.

Coffee mug in hand, he glared at her with an unreadable expression. She couldn't tell if he was simply concerned about her driving skills, or maybe he wanted to be there when she visited the doctor. Beneath the surface, evident in the rigid bearing of his shoulders and the tight grip he had on the mug, he was angry with her.

Well, bully for him! She wasn't all that happy about how their marriage was going, either.

Finally, he shrugged and went back to his place at the table. "Do whatever the hell you want."

She gritted her teeth. The man was impossible.

HER DOCTOR'S appointment went fine; the obstetrician assured her both she and the baby were healthy. She was already taking vitamins, which he encouraged her to continue. His only concern was her distance from the hospital. With a February delivery date, and travel treacherous on winter roads, that could be a problem.

She found a maternity store easily enough and bought three pairs of pants, several tops and a skirt, then lingered at the adjacent baby store. It was too early to begin buying things for the baby, but it did her heart good to finger soft flannel receiving blankets, examine cribs and imagine her baby sleeping there. Her baby and Bryant's.

On the way home she stopped in Reilly's Gulch

to see Sal. A man sitting alone at the bar sipping a beer eyed Ella as she went into Sal's office where the woman was watching her soap opera.

Sal glanced up as the credits rolled. "What brings you into town, honey? I figured you'n Bryant'd still be shacked up enjoying your honeymoon."

Ella smiled weakly. "Everyone has to come up for air occasionally."

Sal's belly laugh bounced around the small room. "I bet that boy is some kind of stud in the sack. He is one gorgeous hunk of man. Could'a been a soap star himself if he'd wanted to go Hollywood."

"Yes, I imagine he could." Though Ella wouldn't want to share him with some pretty little starlet even if that was what the script called for. "I've got my computer up and running, and I'm ready to get started on your bookkeeping system."

Sal elevated her eyebrows in exaggerated surprise. "You're still gonna do that?"

"Of course."

"Does Bryant know?"

"I suppose. I told him when I took the waitress job that I'd be keeping your books, too. I offered to set up his system."

"Funny. I figured Bryant to be one of the old-fashioned guys who wouldn't want his little missus working."

Ella bristled. "I'm hardly a *little missus* and I certainly don't intend to sit around the ranch, twiddling my thumbs and making quilts in my spare time."

"Whatever." Sal lumbered to her feet. "Don't 'spose you doing a little bookkeeping is much different than earning egg money on the side, and it sure 'n hell is a chore I'm happy to pass off to somebody else."

She got out a coffee-stained ledger from the top drawer of her cluttered desk and handed Ella a shoe box full of invoices. "I'm about a month behind in paying bills. Just can't seem to find the time to sit down and do the work."

Smiling to herself, Ella imagined the very last thing Sal would give up in order to make the time would be her soaps.

Just then the one customer who'd been out front stuck his head in the door.

"Hey, Sal, get me another beer, huh? And bring one for your pretty little friend."

Startled, Ella looked at the man in surprise. He was about thirty-five with thinning brown hair he wore in a brush cut, a narrow face and a slender physique. She vaguely remembered seeing him here on the nights she'd waited tables.

"None for me, thanks," she said.

"Get outta here, Bobby. This here is my private office. I'll get you 'nother one, just hold your horses." She shouldered the customer out of the way and headed for the bar.

Bobby lingered by the office door, one hand propped on the doorjamb, his hip cocked suggestively. "You interested in having a good time, sunshine?"

"No, thanks. I'm married." Intentionally turning her back, she began to thumb through Sal's ledger.

Behind her Bobby said, "When you get tired of your ol' man, let me know. I'll show you some fun."

Her skin prickled at the very thought.

When Sal returned, Ella shivered and asked, "Who is that man?"

"Oh, don't let him bother you. That's Bobby Bruhn, Winifred's nephew. Except that he likes to pretend he's still a hotshot Marine, he's mostly all talk and no gumption. Ignore him and he'll move on."

That was exactly what Ella intended to do. Bobby Bruhn gave her the creeps. And raised in the city, she knew a real creep when she met one.

It took Ella a while to figure out Sal's erratic bookkeeping system and sort through the invoices that needed to be paid. Finally she gathered up the materials, tucked Sal's check register under her arm and was ready to head for home.

Except she'd forgotten they needed milk, and she decided to stop at the grocery store to pick up a gallon plus some fresh vegetables.

Chester O'Reilly caught her at the checkout stand. "That's a mighty fine car you've got, young lady."

"Why, thank you." She smiled up at the older gentleman. His hair had thinned and he was slightly stooped, but he carried himself with the same sense of authority that must have served his ancestors well when they had settled this part of the country.

"I'd be interested in buying it from you, miss, if you're ever interested in selling."

Based on Bryant's comments and Arnie at the garage, Chester O'Reilly was the only man in town who had any appreciation for her tiny convertible. "I'll certainly keep that in mind," she told him as she placed a gallon of milk on the cashier's conveyor belt.

She paid her bill and gave a little wave to Chester.

"Now don't you go forgetting, miss," he said. "That's one fine vehicle you've got. Real sporty. Just the thing an old sport like me needs."

She laughed and hurried out to the car. In her heart, she suspected Chester O'Reilly was a lonely man without anything to do. He'd only been making idle conversation, not a serious offer to buy her car.

By the time she drove out of Reilly's Gulch, the sun was dipping low behind the buildup of clouds on the western horizon and Ella knew she'd have to hurry if she was going to have food on the table when Bryant came in for his dinner.

SHE WASN'T *coming back.*

That thought had gnawed at Bryant's gut all day as he and Rusty moved the herd to prevent overgrazing of the north pasture. That was why she'd been so adamant about him not going with her into Great Falls.

Now, as afternoon slipped into evening and he

returned to the ranch, he was afraid his premonition had come true.

Ella wasn't at the house; there was no sign of her car.

How long could a doctor's appointment and a little shopping take?

Her tail wagging, Mollie met him on the back porch and he let the old dog into the house. He hooked his hat on a peg, found the sack of dog food and poured some into Mollie's dish. The kitchen was empty, the counters spotless, the stove cold. He went upstairs to wash up.

Only months after his first marriage, Diane had begun slipping out to see her old boyfriend. Bryant hadn't learned about that until later.

He hadn't expected Ella to quit on him so soon.

Stepping into the shower, he lathered soap on his body, washing out the grime of the day and trying to clean away a cloying sense of failure. Maybe she wasn't going to have his baby at all.

Maybe he'd fallen for another hoax.

He was pulling on a clean pair of jeans when he heard a noise downstairs. He quickly squelched the surge of relief he felt. Their marriage was temporary. Eventually she'd leave—now or later didn't matter.

He paused at the kitchen door. There were grocery sacks on the table and she was bent over, hauling a pan out of the cupboard. His body tightened at the sight of her sweet little rump. He remembered how she'd slept with her rear end nested against his hips. In spite of everything, he wanted to hold her like that again.

She looked up and gave him a hurried smile. "Hi. Sorry I'm late, but I'll have your dinner ready in a jiffy."

"I thought you might not be coming back."

The broiling pan still in her hand, she cocked her head. "Why would you think that?"

"Women have been known to get bored living on a ranch. They find something more interesting to do in town."

"Well, let's see." She placed the pan on the counter, then rummaged through the grocery sacks and came up with a package of lamb chops. "I got poked and prodded by the doctor. He says everything is fine, by the way. Then I was reminded rather dramatically in the maternity shop that I'm still not a perfect size six like my sister and probably won't be in this lifetime."

She fussed with the meat while he watched, finally sliding the pan under the broiler.

"That shouldn't have taken all day." Suspicion flooded his stomach with acid.

"It didn't. I stopped by Sal's on the way home to pick up her records so I can set up a bookkeeping system for her. And then, obviously…" She indicated the groceries on the table. "I stopped by the market to get fresh vegetables and milk. And what's all this heavy-duty questioning about, anyway?"

"Next time you have a doctor's appointment, let me know. I'll drive you into the city."

"Now wait a minute—"

"And I don't want you working for Sal. You're married now. I'll support you."

Her brows shot up, causing her glasses to slide down. She punched them up where they belonged. "What if I *want* to work?"

"Then you can work around the ranch like any rancher's wife would."

"Doing what? I don't know anything about cows. And fixing meals for you and doing the wash isn't exactly a full-time job."

He wasn't being fair to her. He knew it. Until this evening she'd had meals on the table when he came in. His closet was filled with clean clothes, some of which had been mended. The whole house was spotless. She'd even washed the windows. But, damn it, he didn't like the idea of her gallivanting around the countryside, visiting Sal's Hotel, Bar and Grill, where any passing stranger could ogle her.

"If you'd ever lived on a ranch, you'd know what womenfolk were supposed to do."

"*Womenfolk?*" she repeated.

"And that's why you aren't going to last around here, Blondie. You're city through and through."

Smoke began to drift up from the oven vents.

She planted her fists on her hips. "So you think I'm not going to last, huh?"

They stood on opposite sides of the kitchen table, squaring off like two prize fighters in a ring.

"That's what I said."

The smoke from the broiler got a little blacker.

"I'm going to prove you wrong, you know." Her

eyes glistened; her lips tightened into a stubborn line. "I love this ranch."

Mollie barked and scratched at the back door to get out.

"You won't when winter comes, it's twenty below zero and you've been stuck in the house for—"

The smoke alarm went off with a piercing sound.

"No! Not the chops," Ella cried, whirling and grabbing a thin tea towel from the counter.

Bryant cursed. Before he could get to the stove, Ella had already opened the door and grabbed the broiler pan. She tossed the whole mess—chops, grease and all—into the sink and turned on the water.

Smoke, steam and flames boiled up in front of her.

Barking frantically, Mollie tried to scratch her way through the back door.

Shoving Ella aside, Bryant snatched up a small hooked rug from in front of the sink, using it to smother the flames. In seconds he had the fire out.

His heart pounding, he checked on Ella. Her glasses were fogged, her right cheek smudged with soot. Grimacing, she was holding her right hand.

"Are you all right?" he asked.

The alarm continued to shriek.

"That was really stupid of me."

He took her hand, turning it palm up. "You burned yourself pretty badly. We need to run some water on it."

"The lamb chops are a total loss." Her chin trembled.

"No great loss. I've never been much of a sheep man anyway." Using a hot pad—one far thicker than the towel she'd used—he lifted the pan out of the sink and tossed the blackened chops in the trash.

"I'll have to feed you soup for dinner. Nothing else is defrosted."

"Soup is fine." He'd had a lot of nights where soup and sandwiches were all he'd had the energy to fix himself. One more night wouldn't hurt him. "And I'll do the fixing."

She started to object but he hushed her.

He took the time to turn off the shrill fire alarm and let Mollie out so she could calm down.

Then he took Ella's hand and held it under a stream of cold water, the crease between her thumb and finger already beginning to blister. The burn had to hurt like crazy. She'd barely flinched. If anything, the tears in her eyes had been because she was mad at him, then upset that she'd ruined their dinner.

She was one tough lady.

Tough enough to be a Montana rancher's wife?

He didn't want to take any bets on that just yet. But he did wish he hadn't yelled at her, that the memories of Diane's lies hadn't come back to haunt him. Ella deserved better.

"I'm sorry," he said softly as they stood side by side. Almost hidden beneath the smell of burned meat he detected the light trace of her wildflower scent.

"So am I."

He imagined she was apologizing for the burned

dinner. She needn't have. His sins were much greater, including carelessly getting a woman pregnant. He still hadn't had the nerve to tell Cliff that he'd gotten married. There were some questions he wasn't yet ready to answer.

Chapter Ten

Bryant spent most of the next day with a couple of his hired hands fixing a downed drift fence in the south pasture and checking for any signs of rustlers. Another rancher east of town had been hit just two days ago, no clues left behind to help identify the culprits. Bryant had stayed away from the ranch house a lot this past week—avoiding Ella. Little wonder she'd been bored enough to check in with Sal. If Ella wanted to do a little bookkeeping on the side, at least it would keep her occupied, he belatedly realized. He'd have to tell her it was okay with him.

Not that she had listened to him when he'd said it wasn't.

Returning to the ranch house at midafternoon, he spotted her in the backyard. Frowning, he dismounted, tied his horse to the corral fence and walked straight to the back of the house where Ella was—

My God, she was digging up the backyard!

"What the devil are you up to?"

She rested her hands on the shovel. Her face was flushed, sweaty and streaked with dirt, the cockeyed straw hat she was wearing old enough to make a scarecrow look like a pauper.

"A kitchen garden," she said a little breathlessly. "I took the truck into Reilly's Gulch this morning and bought everything I needed from the feed store."

His head snapped toward his truck. He gave it a quick once-over, deciding both Ella and the pickup had survived the trip into town. Then his gaze swung to the back porch steps where Ella had piled bags of fertilizer, flats of tomato plants and packets of vegetable seeds.

"You planning to start a farmer's market?"

"No. I checked and this is what a rancher's wife does—when she isn't doing quilting or baking cakes for church socials. Since, unlike your mother, I'm not very good with crafts, I decided I'd start here first."

"What's my mother got to do with anything?"

"I plan to go to church on Sunday, too. You're welcome to come with me." Using her foot, she thrust the shovel into the hard-packed soil all of about three inches deep and turned over the little bit of dirt she'd managed to dislodge.

Suppressing a grudging smile of respect, he thumbed his hat higher on his forehead. "What about your bookkeeping business?"

She eyed him from under the straw hat. "I'll work on that during the evenings. You've no doubt noticed I don't have anything else to occupy my time at night.''

He could think of something that would keep her plenty busy. Him, too. He wasn't going to suggest it, however. He'd ventured down that path once. If he did it again, he'd never be able to stop.

''Seems a little late in the season to be planting crops,'' he commented as she struggled to poke the shovel deeper into the ground.

She grunted. ''That's why I'm starting the tomatoes as seedlings. Alex at the feed store said the carrots, radishes, onions, beans and corn would be fine. He wasn't so sure about the pumpkins, but I wanted to raise my own—'' she grunted again as she tried to force the shovel deeper ''—jack-o'-lanterns.''

Likely as not, the pumpkins would be covered by snow long before Halloween. ''Must be planning a pretty big garden,'' he said laconically.

''Biggest one in the county. I might just surprise everyone and win some blue ribbons at the county fair.'' She shot him one of her determined looks. ''I plan to can everything we can't eat ourselves.''

When Bryant had been a boy, the Swain family had lived on his mother's canning efforts through most of the winter. He suspected Ella's efforts wouldn't be quite so successful.

''I've always had a special liking for three-inch-long carrots, which is about all you're going to get out of this garden the way you're going.''

''What?''

He closed the distance between them and took

the shovel from her. "You've never raised vegetables, have you?"

"We don't exactly have large yards in Queens. But my mother has two window boxes where she raises herbs to cook with."

"Well, Blondie, if you don't loosen the soil more than you're doing—" he drove the shovel to its full depth into the ground "—your carrots aren't going to be able to grow more than three inches deep. Onions, either."

She closed her eyes, and he could see she was bone weary from the unaccustomed physical work. And she didn't have much to show for her efforts.

"I'll have Shane help you tomorrow," he said in a voice that was oddly low and husky.

She squared her jaw. "I can do it myself."

"You don't have to."

"Yes, I do. I have to prove—"

"My dad always had a hired hand do the hard digging for Mom. She'd do the planting, and my brother and I would be stuck with the weeding."

"Oh."

He lifted her chin, her skin soft and warm in his callused hand. Her eyes were as bright a blue as a wildflower. "Ranch families rely on each other, every member doing what he or she can to help out. That's how it's meant to be."

"City families aren't any different, Bryant. They just don't have as nice a view."

In spite of himself, he had to admire her spunk. She didn't back down for anyone, especially him. He couldn't quite figure out why that was. She didn't have to take the guff he was giving her. She could leave anytime, go back to her job in L.A. or get a new one.

But she'd dug in her heels and wasn't going to budge. He could see that. And there had to be a bigger reason than just keeping up a front for the sake of her family. Ella was too cussedly independent to worry about raising a child on her own unless she had some other agenda.

He simply couldn't figure out what it was.

His gaze slid to her lips. They were slightly full, rosy without the need for lipstick. He remembered their sweet taste. Like strawberries.

She rested her hand on his, her fingers trembling slightly as they curled around the back of his wrist. An acre of Montana dirt had lodged beneath her fingernails; the bandage she'd covered her burn with had come halfway off, the blister dirty and bleeding.

"You should be wearing gloves."

"I forgot to buy any at the store."

"I'll get you some tomorrow." He hadn't kissed her since their wedding. He wanted to now. He wanted to take her upstairs and made love to her in his king-size bed. He wanted to know what changes the baby had made in her body since that first time—since they'd made the baby together.

His baby.

God, he wanted that to be true. But Diane's lie taunted him. He'd been a fool once. Twice a fool and he'd have no one to blame but himself.

He lowered his hand. "You've done enough for

today. Why don't you go get cleaned up? Your vegetable garden will wait until tomorrow.''

He saw a flash of something resembling disappointment in her eyes. He wasn't sure. It could have been just the way the sun glinted off her glasses.

AFTER DINNER that evening he found Ella in his mother's old sewing room where she'd set up her computer. The room's wide expanse of windows and its southern exposure made it the warmest room in the house during the winter; in the summer the west windows caught the afternoon breeze, cooling the room. He and Cliff used to vie for their mother's attention here, distracting her from the prizewinning quilts she made for the county fair.

Until that terrible summer when she'd gotten so sick.

Oddly, it seemed natural that Ella had chosen this room to work in, that she looked very much as if she belonged here. It made it harder to remember she wasn't likely to stay, that their marriage was only a temporary one.

Apparently sensing his presence, she looked up from her work. ''Did you want something?'' she asked.

Yeah, he did. He just didn't dare think he could ask for it.

Giving himself a mental shake, he dragged his thoughts to the reason he'd sought her out. ''I figure you're right about computerizing my records. It's time I stop living in the dark ages when it comes to keeping the books.''

Her smiled sneaked right inside him, warming a lonely spot near his heart.

"Great. I think I'm getting the hang of this book-keeping program I got for Sal. It should be easy to modify it to handle the ranch accounts."

"The quarterly tax returns are due Monday. I've been sweating over the numbers—"

She laughed aloud. "I've got your number, cowboy. You wait until your books are a total disaster and then you turn them over to me to straighten out, and on a deadline yet. Thanks a lot."

He grinned back at her sheepishly. "You've got me pegged all right. Think you can handle it?"

"In my case, it's a lot better than trying to make a quilt. I'm all thumbs when it comes to a needle and thread."

SHE'D SERIOUSLY underestimated the time it would take to set up a bookkeeping system for Bryant. Not only wasn't Ella comfortable yet with the accounting program she'd ordered, keeping track of cows turned out to be a lot different than bottles of booze. It was an inventory nightmare that had her tracking back through dusty records of prior years.

And then, of course, she'd had to enter all the data. No small task on a ranch this big with payrolls and feed bills to manage.

She'd finally cut the tax check for Bryant's signature at midnight Saturday and collapsed into bed. With new admiration for Bryant and what his family had accomplished, she decided retailing was a less complex industry than cattle ranching. Who knew the cost of bull semen could be so high?

Her shoulders still aching from so many hours hunched over the computer, she climbed into Bryant's pickup Sunday morning for their trip into Reilly's Gulch for church.

"You look pretty spiffy," she said as he slid in behind the wheel. He was wearing a sandy-brown western-cut jacket and new jeans. Instead of a tie, he sported a turquoise-and-silver bolo that nicely accented his sky-blue shirt. She didn't know what fashion experts might say, but to her Bryant looked so sexy no woman would be able to resist him. *If* he asked...which, in her case, he hadn't.

She'd been so sure that afternoon in the garden that he was going to kiss her....

"You look pretty good yourself, Blondie."

She fought to suppress the ripple of pleasure his compliment brought her. She hadn't worn a skirt in weeks, and today she'd decided to wear one of her new maternity outfits, a softly flowing blue skirt that reached to midcalf with a cream-colored over-blouse that disguised the telltale swell of her tummy.

"Thanks," she managed to say.

He wheeled the truck out of the long driveway onto the two-lane road that led into town. The morning was a beautiful one, though the heat of summer was already beginning to build.

"After doing your books, it looks to me like the price of beef has been slipping pretty badly the past couple of years," she said as the truck cruised smoothly along the blacktop.

"Tell me about it. The Asian economy tanked and took beef prices with it." His left elbow rested on the windowsill, and he drove with easy confidence. "That's why I was in L.A. in May, talking to the exporter."

And that was when fate had intervened, landing Bryant in his brother's bed the night Ella decided not to die a virgin. "Did you make the deal you wanted?" Which hadn't included matrimony, she imagined.

"Not yet. We're still negotiating."

"You'll have to do something soon. I noticed you have some big loan payments on equipment and stock due in the next quarter."

He glanced in her direction. "After the roundup. If we don't close the deal pretty soon, all the cattlemen around here will have to sell their excess beef on the open market. It'll probably mean losses for everyone."

"The risks of raising cattle, I suppose."

"Yep. Then, assuming we make a profit on this year's beef, all we have to worry about is avoiding a harsh winter that wipes out two-thirds of the herd."

She raised her eyebrows in surprise. "Does that happen often?"

"Only every six or seven years, if we're lucky." He slowed as they reached the outskirts of town. The only business that appeared to be open was Sal's Hotel, Bar and Grill, which had a half-dozen pickups parked out front. "Unfortunately we're about due for another one of those winters."

"I guess every business is a gamble one way or another."

"Do you like to gamble?"

"I'm here, aren't I?" she said a little too quickly.

He turned and she looked him right in the eye. She had an aunt who lived for her Wednesday night bingo games. Ella had taken a far greater risk by coming to Montana and marrying a man she barely knew. Perhaps gambling was in her blood after all.

The church parking lot was nearly full when they arrived. Bryant helped her from the truck, then walked her toward the whitewashed structure where they had been married only weeks ago. His hand was warm where he rested his palm at the small of her back.

There were several clusters of people standing around the entrance visiting, most of them older women. Their conversations came to an abrupt halt as Bryant and Ella drew closer, and all eyes followed them. Bryant tipped his hat to the parishioners. Suddenly nervous, Ella gave them a tentative smile as they entered the vestibule. She'd recognized Winifred Bruhn in the group, notepad in hand—no doubt taking church attendance to report in the weekly newspaper.

"I feel like I've just been paraded past a firing squad," she whispered.

He grinned. "The church ladies are notorious gossips. I imagine whatever they haven't learned about you yet, they'll simply make up."

"None of it good, I suspect," she said grimly. She should have expected the townspeople she hadn't met yet and the neighboring ranchers to be curious about her. By now the news must have spread that she and Bryant had married in haste. Although her figure didn't actually show in her maternity blouse, they'd all begun counting on their fingers, she was sure.

They chose a pew about midway down the aisle. More eyes turned toward them as they took their seats.

Reverend Goodfellow's sermon was both long and loud. Even so, Ella had trouble staying awake. In addition to her pregnancy, she simply wasn't getting enough sleep these days. Surely God had not intended His people to get up before dawn.

As she sat next to Bryant, a sense of contentment stole over her. He'd settled his Stetson on his knees, his fingers idly stroking the brim or measuring the valley he'd formed in the center of the crown. He had nice hands, lean strong fingers. She recalled how gentle he'd been with her the night she'd slipped into his bed.

She wished he'd welcome her there again.

Her body reacted to his closeness, warming as though every cell remembered his touch, the feel of his hands caressing her. His spicy scent triggered memories of him holding her. Kissing her.

It didn't matter that she was in church. Her thoughts were anything but pure. Yet she was his wife, had vowed to honor and cherish him. She intended to keep her promises if Bryant would allow it.

The church service ended with a rousing hymn intended to send the congregation on their way in good spirits—or at least to wake them up after the overly long sermon. Everyone filed out of the church, most stopping to visit once they were outside the door. A light breeze stirred the tops of the poplar trees that lined the parking lot.

"Hello, Bryant, good to see you in church again." The woman who'd greeted them on the church steps was about Ella's age with striking dark eyes, a burnished complexion and hair the shade of midnight.

"'Lo, Candy. How's it going?" Bryant settled his hat squarely on his head.

"The kids keep trying to drive me crazy, but so far I'm winning." With an easy smile, her gaze shifted to Ella. "I hear tell congratulations are in order."

"Thank you," Ella said.

Bryant provided the introductions, then said, "Candy works at Harriet's Beauty Parlor."

"When word spread an outsider had finally led Bryant down the aisle, we single girls in town practically held a wake. A lot of local girls had their eye on him, me included. You've got yourself quite a catch here, Ella." In a gesture of familiarity, Candy rubbed her hand up and down Bryant's arm.

Ella bristled. "Yes, I know."

"Easy, Candy, you don't want Ella getting the wrong—"

"Looks like he didn't waste any time getting you in a family way, honey. Those Swain boys always were fast workers."

A dark-red stain crept up Bryant's neck. "Knock it off, Candy," he grumbled.

"Just wanted to say hello and welcome your missus. You want any haircuts or perms, anything like that, you give me a shout, honey. The girls at the shop will be happy to give you all the low down on this ol' boy, don't you know?"

Ella forcefully held on to her smile, thinking Harriet's Beauty Parlor was the last place she'd ever have her hair done. "I'll remember that," she assured Candy.

Cupping her arm, Bryant eased her away from Candy only to be stopped by a fellow rancher. He made the introductions then chatted awhile, the men commenting about the weather and how well the grass was bearing up under the pressure of grazing.

Ella wasn't bearing up at all well.

Never in her life had she been jealous. She'd had no reason to be. Until now.

She'd bet her 401K that Candy McCloud and Bryant had been intimate. Probably more than once. Which put the beautician a rung or two above Ella on the ladder.

Lord, she shouldn't even be thinking like that. It was none of her business who Bryant had dated or how many of the local women had wanted to marry him. If she hadn't made a serious error in judgment, he'd still be free to sleep with anyone he cared to. She'd still be a virgin. She wouldn't be carrying his child. She wouldn't have fallen in love with the father of her baby.

Instinctively, her hand slid across her tummy. That was one thing she'd never regret, having Bryant's child. She could easily imagine his features on an infant's face, his long lashes framing sparkling blue eyes, his quick smile.

She got into the truck, primly folding her hands in her lap as she waited for Bryant to climb in behind the wheel. Her blister showed signs of healing and calluses were beginning to form on her palms. No amount of scrubbing could remove all the dirt from under her nails.

Maybe soon Bryant would begin to think her suitable to be a rancher's wife.

"I gather you and Candy have been friends for a long time." She kept her eyes forward so he wouldn't detect how troubled the conversation had left her.

"We went to school together."

"You dated her?"

"Yeah. We went out a couple of times." He waited for a car to pass before he edged the truck into the line exiting the church parking lot.

"Did you—" She clamped her mouth shut. It was none of her business.

Reaching across the cab, he placed his hand on her thigh. "Every girl in our class except one was married by the September following graduation. Candy married Tim McCloud. I was happy for her and I'm sorry it didn't work out. But our dating is ancient history."

She slanted Bryant a glance. "Who was the one?"

"Yvonne Butterworth. She married my brother the day after he graduated from college."

"It must have been terrible for him when she died."

"It was, and I think he's still afraid to get too close to any woman. But at least he has his son."

"Yes, Stevie's adorable." And Ella was grateful her uncharacteristic spark of jealousy had been unfounded. Bryant's heart was hers to win—or lose—all on her own.

AS THE HEAT of August began to crescendo, the corn wilted under the unrelenting sun and the tomato plants drooped. Every day Bryant noted signs that Ella was struggling to keep her garden growing. She watered the rows of vegetables by hand, making sure the ground remained damp. She weeded and spread fertilizer.

Earlier in the month she'd proudly presented him with a plateful of radishes she'd grown, far more than an army could eat all at once. Most of them she'd had to throw out. And then had come an equal number of carrots prepared fresh, creamed, in stews and stir fried until Bryant was sure they both were overdosing on vitamin A and their skin would turn yellow.

The beans she'd planted had been invaded by a meal bug; worms were attacking the tomatoes on the vine. Ella fought back, her squeamish distaste of those green worms almost funny except she was so damn serious about her garden.

Everything she did, she did with stubborn determination. He'd come to admire that trait in her. He remembered she'd made love with the same fierce spirit even though she'd been a novice.

By September he had the hands moving the cattle from summer pasture back to the home valley, closer to the ranch house where he could keep track of them during the winter, hauling feed to them as necessary. All the men, Bryant included, spent grueling hours on horseback covering ten miles or more a day. The bulls seemed especially unruly this year, unwilling to be herded away from their favorite grazing areas.

It was late in the day when he, Rusty and Shane were bringing in about twenty head of strays they'd rounded up, three of them big ol' bulls with huge shoulders and mean dispositions. They had to pass near the ranch house to get them linked up to the main herd.

He touched his heels to his horse's flanks, his favorite cowpony. The gelding responded with a burst of speed to force a wandering heifer back into line.

"Keep 'em away from the ranch, Shane," he yelled at the boy working the other side of the herd.

Shane waved an acknowledgment.

Bryant shifted in his saddle to check on Rusty, who was riding drag.

He didn't see what happened, but the next thing he knew a couple of bulls had veered away from the small herd, running hard toward the ranch house. Spooked, the cows started after them. Their hooves stirred up a cloud of dust.

Bryant dug his heels into the horse and bent low over the gelding's neck. His angle on the runaway cows was all wrong. If he was going to turn the stampede before the cattle got too close to the ranch house and out buildings, he had to get ahead of the lead bull. The way they were running, he didn't have much of a chance.

He'd about decided to pull up, let the cattle run themselves out and hope they didn't do too much damage, when he caught a glimpse of someone working in the garden behind the house.

Ella!

She didn't know the cattle were coming, hadn't heard them yet.

He swore and whipped his cowpony with the reins.

Damn, why couldn't she hear the stampede? Feel the rumble of pounding hooves shaking the earth beneath her feet?

He saw her look up—finally—then freeze.

"Get into the house!" he shouted, but she couldn't possibly hear him.

He was helpless to do anything. His horse couldn't overtake the lead animals. They had too big a head start. He could only hope Ella had enough sense to get herself to safety. The low, wood railing fence around the backyard had never been intended to ward off a stampede.

She started to move—the wrong direction! Toward the rampaging cattle.

"No!" he shouted.

She waved her silly straw hat at the cows and he could hear her screams over the sound of the bawling animals.

"Damn city girl!" he muttered, still trying to get his mount in position to head off the herd.

He didn't make it.

The lead animals burst through the fence as if it were made of toothpicks, the cattle trampling everything in their path. Dust and bits of vegetation flew into the air, obscuring the scene.

Risking both his horse and his own hide, he cut through the herd. Fear was a living thing, tearing at his gut and clogging his throat.

Once he was on the other side of the cattle, he wheeled his horse to a stop, pulled his rifle from its scabbard and pulled off three shots into the air. The frightened cows bawled even more loudly and turned away from the house.

Bryant's lungs seized on the dust and dirt, and he coughed, phlegm filling his throat. He turned, his gaze searching across the trampled vines and rows of corn.

In the middle of the garden there was a mound barely larger than a child would make, the pastel pattern of her blouse spattered with mud. She lay there unmoving, curled into a ball, her arms wrapped protectively around her stomach.

"Ella!" he cried, dismounting and racing to her side.

Chapter Eleven

Like flying shrapnel, dirt clods had pummelled Ella. Three-foot-high cornstalks lay draped over her in a crazy, pick-up-sticks pattern.

Kneeling, Bryant ripped away the debris. He touched her gently, felt for her pulse and found it racing more wildly than his own.

"Thank God," he murmured. Even the surge of relief he felt wasn't enough to drain all the adrenaline from his veins. *She was alive.*

Slowly her eyes opened.

"Don't move," he warned. "You may have some broken bones."

"I tried to—" She coughed and blinked. "They…ruined everything."

"Don't worry about the garden. We can always buy vegetables at the store." He wiped mud from her face and pulled a tomato vine from her hair. From head to toe, she looked as if she'd been mud wrestling…and had lost the first round. He'd never met a more courageous woman—or one more foolhardy. "Do you hurt anywhere? Were you stepped on?"

She struggled to sit up. Her eyes filled with tears and she adjusted her glasses. "All I wanted to do was prove—"

"Shh, you don't have to prove anything. Easy now."

Wincing a little, she got into a sitting position and tried to brush the dirt from her blouse. Her hand came away muddy. "I'm a mess. Those stupid cows…" She drew a shuddering breath that turned into a sob and tears spilled down her cheeks. From all appearances she seemed more shaken than broken.

An emotion so powerful he didn't know how to name it filled Bryant's chest. More than relief. Beyond gratitude.

Gingerly, he slid his arms beneath her, lifting her gently to cradle her against his chest. She buried her head on his shoulder. She felt slight and vulnerable, yet she'd had the valor to stand her ground against a stampeding herd of cattle—all to protect her precious vegetable garden. How much more would she do to protect someone she loved?

Rusty came riding into the yard and reined his cowpony to a hard stop. "Me 'n' the boy got the herd settled. How's the missus? She hurt?"

"She'll be all right." Bryant said the words as much to reassure himself as his foreman. "I'm taking her inside. See if you and the hands can clean up some of this mess."

She clung to him as he carried her to the house.

Her gardening tools had been scattered around, the hoe broken in three pieces, a flowerpot filled with geraniums shattered. It could have as easily been her body that fractured beneath the trampling hooves.

Without pausing, he carried her upstairs and into the master bathroom, remodeled with fancy tile and a big shower stall the year he'd married Diane. He lowered Ella to her feet.

"Can you stand on your own?" he asked.

"I'm fine." She fought her tears as fiercely as she had tried to wave off the bulls with that ridiculous straw hat. "Bruised, maybe."

"Let's check you out." He wanted to see for himself that she was all in one piece, that the damage done was more to her stubbornness than to herself…or the baby she carried.

He started to lift the hem of her blouse.

"I can manage." She trembled, shivering from the wet, cold mud that covered her. She shivered in anticipation, too. The wanting that had plagued her since that night so long ago when he'd made love to her stirred again, making her ache with longing. Her knees went weak and she leaned into him. She wanted so much for him to hold her, to make everything all right. She was so tired of trying to be a rancher's wife, to prove she had the right stuff.

"Shh, Blondie," he whispered, his voice caressing her, his private name for her rippling warmly across her awareness. "I've got you." With ease, he pulled her top off over her head.

"Please…" Her throat clogged on a sense of

failure, that she'd never be good enough to be a rancher's wife.

He placed a kiss on the juncture of her neck and shoulder, a tender place grazed by a flying hoof. "We need to get you cleaned up," he whispered.

The husky timbre of his voice sent tingles down her spine, and need curled more tightly through her belly. He slid her elastic-waist jeans down over her hips.

"Sit here," he ordered. He knelt in front of her when she sat on the closed lid of the stool, then removed her muddy shoes before tugging off her pants.

Embarrassed heat shot to her cheeks. He hadn't seen her since that night, since her tummy had begun to expand with her pregnancy.

He placed his hand on her stomach. Lovingly. His palm warmed through the skimpy fabric of her underwear.

"The baby? He's okay?"

She nodded, his gentleness bringing tears to her eyes again. "I curled into a ball so the cows wouldn't—"

"I know. I saw you."

He examined her with exquisite care, his blue eyes darkening to navy as his gaze explored her body. The bruise he found on her thigh he kissed tenderly. He provided equal attention to a scrape he discovered on her hip. Removing her bra, he provided even more compassionate attention to her breasts, weighing them in his palms, brushing his tongue over the nipples, although there was no sign of injury.

Deep inside, Ella's body clenched in response. She moaned softly.

"Am I hurting you?"

Unable to speak, she shook her head.

"Let's get you in the shower and get the mud washed off. I want to be sure…" His voice caught, and he stepped away to turn the water on, then stripped his shirt off. His muscles rippled as he quickly shed his boots and pants, revealing he was as aroused as she.

Fear and anxiety warred within her along with excitement. Surely he intended to make love to her, to take this intimate moment one step further. For weeks she'd wanted this to happen, to have Bryant want her for more than a marriage in name only. For more than simply giving their baby his name. If it took a stampeding herd of cattle to push him beyond the point of no return, she'd willingly stand her ground against every charging bull in the county.

But what if they made love and in her inexperience he found her inadequate? Found that she wasn't sexy enough. Perhaps she lacked what it took to satisfy a man so thoroughly masculine as Bryant and that was why he'd been willing to forego the physical pleasures of marriage.

She shuddered as he drew her to her feet. Her nerves tangled, her breathing stumbled.

"You won't be needing these," he said as he

carefully removed her glasses and set them on the counter before they entered the shower together.

He was right. Seeing was redundant when she was enveloped by such potent tactile sensations. His hands covered her, soaping her body, lathering shampoo into her hair. His fingers tunneled through her hair, kneading her scalp, raising goose bumps along her spine despite the warm water cascading down her back.

In return, her fingers caressed him, given full rein at last to explore the contours of his chest, the soft mat of hair that grew thicker at the base of his arousal, which sprang powerfully upward. She cupped him, and a deep groan vibrated through his chest.

"Ella…" His arms closed around her, possessing her. Her body, slick with soap, molded against his. When his mouth claimed hers, she tasted his urgency, a need that was as powerful as her own. She responded eagerly to his plunging, searching tongue.

He murmured sweet words of praise—to her courage, to her femininity; her breathing grew rapid and she kissed him again, thrilling to the onslaught to her senses. Thrilling to Bryant's touch, his kisses, the caress of his callused hands and the soft spill of water across her bare flesh.

When the water grew chill, he wrapped her in big, thick towels and carried her into the bedroom. He lay down with her on his massive bed, pulling her once again into his arms. He stroked her, caressing her again as though he hadn't already explored every sensitive inch of her flesh.

"I don't want to hurt you," he whispered. "The baby—"

"Is fine. You won't hurt us."

His finger dipped into her soft, feminine folds. She bucked against his hand and he teased the nub there until she was moaning, writhing beneath his touch and aching for more.

"Please…" she whispered.

When his finger slid inside her, she felt her own dampness close around him. He teased and aroused her until she was desperate, crying out his name.

Only then did he position himself above her, probing the heart of her femininity. Lifting her hips, she opened herself to him. Her body. Her heart. On a sob, his name wrenched free from deep in her soul.

"Yeah, I'm here, sweetheart," he murmured softly.

Then he was inside her, stretching her, filling her. She cried his name again as she plummeted over a precipice. A moment later, she felt him join her in his own explosive moment that was like a star burst, spectacular in its vivid colors yet doomed to return to earth.

Bryant fought to keep his full weight from collapsing on her, the feeling of being totally drained making him weak. He hadn't intended to make love to her. But from the moment he'd carried her upstairs, his adrenaline still flowing with the fear that she might be seriously injured, he hadn't been able to stop himself. He might never be able to stop himself again.

He rolled off her, falling back onto his pillow with a groan. The scent of soap and shampoo lingered in the air, mixing with the fragrance of mind-bending sex. The combination was indelible. Something he'd not soon forget.

But he also couldn't forget Ella could still leave him. Winter was still a month or more off. A city girl could hate the remoteness of his ranch, could feel trapped by the long cold days yet to come. Could leave in a second, taking her baby with her.

His baby.

After all, she'd never asked for more than a temporary marriage.

In frustration, his hands balled into fists. There was nothing he could do to prevent her leaving. He could only protect himself by not caring too much.

CONFLICTING EMOTIONS and hours of sleeplessness drove Ella from Bryant's bed before his alarm went off. After they'd made love, she'd draped her arm across his chest, cuddling against him, only to feel him tense.

The languid, contented feeling that had filled her vanished in an instant, making her wonder what had gone wrong. What had *she* done wrong?

A full measure of old insecurities had come cascading back on her. She'd squeezed her eyes closed, willing the tears that threatened to stay away. She didn't doubt she'd satisfied him physically. But any woman could do that.

Where she'd failed was in touching his heart in the same way he'd long since claimed hers.

In the predawn darkness she slipped out of his room and went to her own across the hall, where she dressed.

Downstairs, Mollie met her at the kitchen door, her tail wagging.

"Did we forget to feed you last night, girl?" Ella's stomach rumbled as she petted the dog. Distracted by their lovemaking, she and Bryant had skipped dinner, too. She'd also failed to work on the books for O'Reilly's Feed Store, her latest accounting client. Chester O'Reilly had badgered his sons into hiring her, bringing to three the number of businesses she was handling, including the ranch.

Smiling wryly as she poured Mollie's food into her dish, Ella decided she was having more success as a bookkeeper than as a rancher's wife. Sadly, that seemed to be the story of her life.

She put the coffee on, then stepped out onto the back porch as the first trace of dawn caused the stars to fade. In the pale light she could see that the trampled fence had been repaired; uprooted tomato plants and cornstalks were piled in one corner of the yard.

Next year...

Emotion clogged her throat. How could she possibly stay as Bryant's wife if he couldn't find it in his heart to return the love she was so ready to give?

She heard a noise in the kitchen, saw Bryant's shadow move across the window.

However glorious their interlude had been, nothing had changed between them.

Digging deep, she found the well of her stubborn pride. She wouldn't let him know how much she wished it were otherwise.

Lifting her chin, she went back into the kitchen. Her breath caught at the first sight of him, the way his shirt tugged across his shoulders, his jeans hugged his hips as he stood pouring his first cup of coffee. She swallowed hard, determined not to reveal the depth of her feelings. The well of insecurities that threatened to engulf her.

"Rusty and the boys did a good job of cleaning up the yard." Without meeting his gaze, she got the milk and eggs from the refrigerator and a bowl from under the counter. "I'll make you pancakes. You must be hungry. I know I'm starved. In case you didn't notice, we skipped dinner last night."

For a long heartbeat, he was silent, then said, "I noticed."

She measured a double portion of pancake mix. Her hand trembled slightly, and she dusted the counter with flour. "It'll just take me a minute."

"Ella…"

Gathering herself, she turned and met his gaze steadily.

"About what happened yesterday…"

She wanted to say something clever, to come up with a "morning-after" witticism to ease the tension that had her nerves on edge. But she couldn't find her voice. His eyes were a dark-blue, his expression so intense it burrowed into her awareness, swamping her with confusion. What was he thinking?

The moment spun out like threads of cotton candy, sweet and fragile.

"Yeah," he finally drawled, his voice low and rough. Looking away, he broke the connection. "Pancakes would be good."

Whatever he'd intended to say was lost. Just like the moment. Just like her heart, Ella thought sadly.

BRYANT STAYED OUT of the house the rest of the day. He mended tack that didn't need fixing, mucked out stalls even though that was the job of his hired hands.

He didn't know what to say to Ella. How could he tell her making love had been a mistake when it had felt so damn good? How could he explain he didn't want them to get too close? That he was scared spitless she'd leave him and take the baby with her?

A man couldn't say those things so he said nothing at all. It was safer that way.

Rusty sauntered into the barn and rested his arms on the stall railing. "Reckon the hay crop will be ready for cuttin' next week?"

"Oughtta be."

"Yep, that's what I figured." He took off his hat, scratched at his fringe of red hair, and settled his hat again, watching Bryant shovel the manure into a wheelbarrow.

Bryant glared at him. "You got somethin' else on your mind?"

"No, not me. It's jus' that you ain't done any mucking since yore daddy made you 'n' Cliff partners in the Double S. Figured you might wanna talk or something."

"You figured wrong."

"If you say so, son, but I been around long enough to spot a man who's hidin' out cuz of woman troubles. You wanna talk, you jus' let me know."

"Yeah, I'll do that. *If* I wanna talk."

After a while, when Bryant continued to ignore him, Rusty wandered off. Bryant kept puttering around the barn until it was almost dinnertime. He'd either have to go inside pretty soon or eat with the hands at the bunkhouse.

Using one more delaying tactic, he got in his truck and drove to the highway to check the mailbox. There was a letter for Ella from her mother, a couple of bills and an envelope with the return address of the Asian exporting company. He ripped that envelope open first.

"Damn," he muttered, reading the letter a second time.

By the time he got back to the ranch house, Ella was ready to put dinner on the table. He washed up at the sink and sat down.

"I take it from your grim expression the herd has been infected with mad cow disease," she said teasingly as she put a plate of chicken and gravy in front of him.

"Close enough. The mail came." He shoved the letter from her mother across the table and handed her the one from the exporter. Since Ella was already handling the bookkeeping, he didn't have any financial secrets.

Sinking into her chair, she looked at the exporter's letter first.

"I'm sorry, Bryant. I know how much you were counting on that contract."

"Me and a lot of other folks in Reilly's Gulch."

"Does this mean—" She placed the letter on the table as though she didn't want to hold it a minute longer than necessary. "Will you lose the ranch?"

"No, not this year. We're not all that far in debt. The bank will extend our loans for another year."

"But if the Asian situation doesn't change by next year you'll still be in the same fix and you'll owe twice as much."

"That's how this business goes. Two or three good years and then the bottom drops out." He cut into his chicken and took a big bite. This was his favorite meal, chicken and gravy piled on top of mashed potatoes. He suspected it was a peace offering from Ella, but she wasn't the one in the wrong. He was.

"What about Cliff? Could he pay off some of the debt from his—"

"It's *my* job to run the Double S. All the money the ranch makes goes back into the business. This year it'll be zip, nada."

"But with the increased interest—"

"Forget it. I'm not asking Cliff for anything. He's got his own mortgage to pay and a kid to raise. I'll sell off some of the steers at market price."

She studied her meal in silence, poking at her mashed potatoes with her fork. "I have some money, Bryant. Not a whole lot, I admit. The move up here cost me—"

"I don't want your money, either. The ranch isn't going to go under. We'll get by. I'll see to that. We just have to tighten our belts a little."

"But it only makes good business sense to—"

He slammed down his fork and knife, silencing her. He was upset with himself that the Asian deal hadn't gone through—and that he wanted to forget dinner, take Ella upstairs to his bed and make love to her all over again. He was becoming an emotional basket case. She had that effect on him. She had since that first time she'd climbed into *Cliff's* bed.

Ah, hell! He didn't know what to do, so he shoved back from the table, then hid out in his den, pretending to study the printouts she'd given him of the ranch's accounts.

But that was a lie.

All he was really thinking about was Ella and how much he wanted her again.

He finally went upstairs to crawl into bed alone. He'd barely turned the light off when the hall door opened and she slipped inside, walking as lightly into the room as a dream.

The mattress shifted when she slid under the covers beside him. His whole body reacted with a force that had him gasping for air; his arms trembled with the effort it took not to embrace her, to drag her closer and never let her go. His mind reeled with conflicting desires.

"Ella…"

"Shh. Let's not talk."

Her lips covered his and he couldn't find the will-power to send her away.

Chapter Twelve

When Bryant came in for supper the following evening, Ella was at the stove, hamburgers sizzling in the frying pan. He headed for the sink to clean up and came to a halt midstride. A pile of hundred-dollar bills lay at his place on the kitchen table.

"What's that?" he asked.

She glanced over her shoulder. "I know we're living in a credit-card economy, but it must have gone further than I had realized if you don't recognize real money when you see it."

"I know it's money." Several thousand dollars' worth, he'd guess, if all the bills were hundreds. "I want to know what it's doing on the table."

"The money's for you, Bryant." She set her spatula aside and turned to face him. "You can pay off part of your outstanding loans with it, which would be the smart thing to do in order to reduce the ranch's interest expense. Or you can burn it. Your choice."

His eyes narrowed. "I told you I didn't want—"

"I heard you loud and clear. But I'm your wife—

at least temporarily—and as you once informed me, family members help each other out. That's what I'm doing.''

Temporarily. God, it hurt to have her say the word aloud, like a punch in the gut. But that was what they'd agreed to, both of them.

In spite of himself, Bryant picked up the money and riffled through the bills. "Where did you get this much money? You didn't cash in your retirement account, did you?" The tax penalty for that would be substantial.

"I sold my car to Chester O'Reilly."

His head snapped up. "You what?"

"Unlike some other people around here, Chester greatly admired my convertible and thought it was just the thing to put a little youth back into his life. He agreed to take over my remaining payments and gave me the difference in cash for my asking price. I have the feeling he's going to start a Reilly's Gulch taxi and tour-guide service." Behind her glasses, her blue eyes sparkled with amusement.

The humor of old Chester running a taxi service, and never driving faster than ten miles an hour, almost made Bryant forget his resentment. Ella was trying to bail him out—and he needed to stifle his pride and accept her money. He'd been sweating his financial problems all day and hadn't known where to turn.

She'd given him the answer, though it hurt to admit that.

"When you leave, you'll need a car," he said softly.

Her expression crumbled. She opened her mouth to speak, then turned back to the hamburgers. "I'll worry about that when the time comes."

He ached to go to her, to pull her into his arms and thank her for what she'd done. She'd sacrificed her ridiculous car, her pride and joy, for him and the Double S. But the words lodged in his throat; his boots felt nailed to the floor. No woman had worried about him in a very long time, not since his adoptive mother had died.

Fingering the money, he did some mental arithmetic. "With this I'll be able to keep the herd intact and not sell off so many head this fall."

Her back still to him, she nodded. "Dinner's almost ready if you want to wash up."

"I'll pay you back," he said, hating himself that he had to accept her help. The Swains had left the ranch in his care. He should be able to manage on his own. But the vagaries of the market place...

"You'd better wash. There's nothing worse than cold hamburgers."

"Right." He swallowed his pride in a painful gulp. "I'll go put the money in the safe and then..." He let the words trail off, wishing there was a way to express his gratitude and yet not have to speak the words he was afraid she'd rebuff.

He didn't dare put a name to the emotions he was feeling, the tightness that filled his chest every time he thought about her leaving—and taking the baby with her.

SEPTEMBER AND EARLY October were filled with the work of thinning the herd and shipping beef to market at deflated prices that only marginally covered costs and drained all hope of a profit for local cattlemen. Bryant heard of rustling activity south of town, another blow to the ranchers. He kept his cowhands on alert, in the saddle for long hours every day patrolling his land, and the Double S escaped without any raids on the herd.

At night he was bone weary when he climbed into bed, happy to seek the comfort of Ella's arms when she joined him there. Neither of them had spoken of changing their arrangement; her clothes were still hanging in the guest room. But every night, even when he was too tired to do anything but sleep, she cuddled against him and he inhaled her wildflower scent. He told himself not to get used to her being there. She could leave. He had no real hold on her.

But that insistent voice of caution grew weaker with each passing day.

Ella groaned next to him and shifted her position in bed.

"What's wrong?" he asked sleepily.

"Nothing. Junior's just practicing a little bronc riding at my expense." She took Bryant's hand, placing his palm on her belly, swollen now with more than five months of pregnancy.

For a moment he felt nothing except the seductive warmth of her flesh through her cotton nightgown. Then something stirred, the subtle press of a tiny fist against his palm, or maybe a foot. He closed his eyes, picturing the baby growing inside her. The doctor had said it was a boy. Until now, until he had felt the baby stir in her womb, it hadn't seemed real.

His son.

He tugged her nightgown above her waist. Bending, he placed a gentle kiss on her soft flesh right where he'd felt the baby move. Dear God, how could he let his son go? Or this determined, stubborn woman who would give birth to his child?

THE FIRST SNOW fell in mid-October.

Still in her robe and slippers, Ella dragged Bryant out to the front porch. ''Look, isn't it beautiful?'' She inhaled deeply of the crisp, cool air, letting her gaze sweep across the open countryside. The beauty astounded her, the subtle changes in the landscape.

The rising sun tinted the patches of snow a faint shade of pink, the scant covering of ice crystals so thin the golden-brown grass of summer still peeked through. The entire scene was like a pastel watercolor.

''In this part of the country, we don't bother to measure a few little patches of snow like that,'' Bryant said, humoring her.

''It still counts as the first snowfall of the year,'' she said stubbornly, grinning up at him. He'd pulled on his jeans and boots; his flannel shirt hung open, his white T-shirt pulling tautly across his broad chest.

''You aren't likely to be so thrilled by snow when it reaches six feet and we have to tunnel our way to get to the barn to feed the animals.''

"That will be beautiful, too. I *love* snow. Every year after the Christmas rush at my father's menswear store, the family would go up to Vermont to ski. It was great."

He shook his head. "This won't be the same, Blondie."

Refusing to let him quash her good spirits, she danced down the steps, found a suitable patch of snow and mashed it into a ball. Whirling, she let fly a perfect throw, smacking him right in the chest. Bits of the snowball clung to his white T-shirt.

He stood stock-still on the porch, staring at her openmouthed, then his eyes narrowed.

She backed away. "You said this didn't count as snow. Logically it follows that was a non-snowball I threw at you."

In slow, measured steps he walked down the stairs.

"Now, Bryant..." She retreated another few feet, a giggle threatening, and placed her hand on the obvious swell of her tummy. "Remember my delicate condition."

"Delicate, my foot!" he said with a growl. Bending, he scooped up some snow, forming a snowball three times the size of the one she'd thrown at him.

"That's not fair. Your hands are bigger than mine."

"I guess I hadn't mentioned the Swain boys' famous battle at Reilly's Gulch Elementary School. My brother and I built a snow fort and held off the entire student body for six hours. It's in the record book."

Swallowing hard, she looked for an escape route. There wasn't one. "No, I guess you didn't mention that."

"Our most effective strategy was to attack our opponents when they weren't expecting it."

"Really. How interesting." She edged off the walkway, trying for a dash to the back door. "You know, it's really cold out here. I think I'll—"

He didn't let her finish. In a few quick strides he was on her, his arm snaring her around her waist. She expected to get a snowball in the face. Instead, grinning like a schoolboy, he slipped it down her back.

She screamed and laughed, squirming to get away from him and the freezing-cold snowball. He didn't let her go, but held her hard against the breadth of his chest.

Suddenly, inexplicably, his mood changed, the teasing laughter vanished and he was kissing her deeply, his lips warming hers. She leaned into him. His arousal pressed against her belly and need curled through her midsection.

"Bryant?"

Before she could protest too forcefully, he lifted her in his arms and carried her inside, upstairs to his bed where he made exquisite love to her until the sun had melted much of the snow that had fallen during the night.

A WEEK LATER, a foot of snow covered the ground. In order to cut expenses, Bryant laid off all of his hired hands except Shane and Rusty.

The ranch was ready to face the long months of winter, the time when isolation tested even the strongest of those who chose to live on this unforgiving land.

In his heart, Bryant still questioned that Ella had the will to endure the harsh environment. Or if she would want to.

"I ADMIT IT. Picking out a Christmas tree on the corner lot in Queens is a heck of a lot easier than this." Ella tramped through the snow behind Bryant, sinking to her knees in the drifts, each new step a challenge. Despite her fur-lined boots, her feet were like blocks of ice and her glasses kept fogging up. "But do we have to check out *every* tree in the forest?"

"Old Swain family custom. You can go back to the truck and wait, if you'd like."

She stopped. Breathing hard, she planted her fists on her hips. "If Swain women freeze off their toes every Christmas in an effort to find the single best tree in the woods, then by God, I'll do it, too. But I have to tell you, I *really* liked that tree we saw right next to where you parked the truck."

Lowering his ax from his shoulder, he studied the tree in front of him. "That's what my mother always used to tell my dad."

"Smart lady."

He began circling the tree under examination. "Of course, Dad never listened to her. We had to check out every tree we could find."

"Stubbornness must run in the family."

"It's a learned trait. I remember our first Christmas on the ranch. Cliff and I were five years old. I don't think we'd ever had a tree of our own."

"You weren't born on the Double S?" she asked in surprise. Given his love of the land, she'd assumed the ranch had always been his home.

He glanced in Ella's direction, but from the look in his eyes she thought he was probably seeing into the past.

"My brother and I were abandoned by our birth mother. She left us sitting on a church pew and the priest found us sleeping there the next morning."

Ella drew in a sharp breath, the cold air chilling her lungs in the same way Bryant's admission chilled her heart. She couldn't imagine what would drive a woman to abandon her own children.

"We were in foster care for a long time, first while they were looking for our mother and then because not a lot of people wanted to adopt twins. The authorities didn't want to separate us." Idly he tested the branch of the fir with his gloved fingers, checking the needles as they sprang back in his hand. "When the Swains brought us to the ranch, it was shortly before Christmas. Cliff and I were convinced Santa Claus would never be able to find us way out here."

"But Santa did find you."

Bryant's lips twitched into a lopsided smile. "I'll say. Dad insisted we pick out the biggest tree we could find so Santa would have plenty of room under it for his presents. When Christmas morning came and Santa had left so much stuff just for the two of us, we figured he had pretty well emptied his entire sleigh. We started to worry then that no other kids in the whole world had gotten any toys.''

Despite a smile, Ella's throat tightened and tears burned at the backs of her eyes. She imagined those two little boys, so desperate for Santa to find them. Her heart ached for them and for the wounds they had suffered.

Now she understood why Bryant only wanted their marriage to be a *temporary* one. He'd been abandoned by his biological mother and then by the young wife he'd married. In death, even his adoptive mother had left him, too. No wonder he was leery of commitment and afraid to trust another woman with his heart.

How could Ella convince him that she wouldn't be like those other women, that she wouldn't abandon him if he gave her some other choice?

He tipped his hat farther back on his head. ''Now that I think of it, that tree by the truck was a pretty good one.''

''Probably the best in the whole county,'' she heartily agreed, wondering how fast the truck heater could warm up the cab—and her ice-cold feet.

''What do you say we go cut it down?''

''I'd say that's a really good idea.'' She walked beside him as they headed back toward the truck, linking her arm through his. Abandoned as he had been, surely he wouldn't easily give up his own son.

Neither would she.

Nor would she give up hope of capturing Bryant's wary heart.

CHRISTMAS DAY dawned clear and cold.

To Ella's delight, Santa hadn't failed the Swain family this year. Not another present could have been squeezed beneath the tree and most of them were for the baby—a crib with matching sheets and bumper pads, a musical cowboy mobile that played "Home on the Range" and a huge teddy bear. Though they had promised not to go overboard on gifts for each other, given the ranch's financial situation, she had given Bryant a pair of lined leather gloves to replace the worn ones he'd been wearing. In return he'd given her a pastel wool sweater that he said would make her eyes an even deeper shade of blue.

"Thank you," she said, hugging the sweater. Sitting on the floor amid an avalanche of torn and crumpled wrapping paper, she leaned back against the couch. Mollie wiggled across the room on her stomach to rest her grizzled chin on Ella's thigh. Absently she ran her fingers through the dog's thick fur. "I can't remember a nicer Christmas."

"You must be missing your folks."

"A little. I'll call them later after I get the turkey in the oven." With the bunkhouse practically emptied of ranch hands, Rusty and Shane had taken to eating most of their dinners with Bryant and Ella. Sal would be joining them for the Christmas celebration. "How about your brother?"

Bryant tossed some crumpled paper into the fireplace and laid another log in the hearth. "I'll call pretty soon. Since his wife died, holidays have been hard on Cliff and Stevie. They're probably just as happy to be someplace else where the memories aren't so strong."

Remembering the schoolteacher Cliff had been dating last summer, she said, "Maybe he'll find someone soon."

"Not very likely in L.A. City girls don't do well up here in Montana."

She bristled. "That's like saying all cowboys are ignorant. It's not necessarily so."

"Sure it is." He shot her a wicked grin. "But women are so taken with our sex appeal, they forget to check out our intellect."

"Oh, you..." Laughing, she tossed a wad of wrapping paper at him. Mollie gave a quick bark, then settled down again.

What on earth could Ella do to prove his bias against city-bred women was wrong? How could she show, once and for all, that she had the right stuff to be his wife...forever?

Chapter Thirteen

As the new year began, temperatures plummeted. That was followed by wave after wave of storm clouds that dumped increasing amounts of snow on the landscape.

Bryant had been right. Just getting to the barn became a dangerous ordeal.

By the end of the month, between the subzero temperatures and the depth of the snow, the Double S was at risk of losing a large part of the herd.

Ella slid the remaining two pancakes from the griddle onto her plate. Outside the frosted kitchen window, dawn was little more than watery gray light. They'd had snow again last night, but the overcast would keep the temperature above zero, a small respite from the biting cold of the past week.

"We're going to have to haul hay out to the herd today," Bryant said, pouring himself a second cup of coffee.

Sitting at the table finishing his serving of pancakes, Rusty nodded his agreement. "They'll be needing it by now, that's for sure. Snow's deep enough to bury a pile of cows standing ten high.''

''Then how on earth will you take anything to the cattle?'' Ella asked, sitting down opposite the ranch foreman. ''You and Shane can hardly make it here from the bunkhouse and then only because you put up those guide ropes.'' The thought of going outside at all gave her the chills. To be out in the weather for as long as it would take to deliver hay to even the closest cows seemed impossible, an invitation to frostbite or worse.

''That's what we gotta do more years than not,'' Rusty assured her.

Shane finished the pancakes on his plate and looked up expectantly. The youth was either growing like a weed or he had a hollow leg. She kept doubling the amount of food she usually prepared and still he kept asking for more.

Smiling, she levered herself back to her feet, her expanding belly making everything she did a little awkward. Only a couple of weeks to go until her due date and she'd begun to suffer from a recurring backache. Not an unusual problem for a woman whose stomach preceded her by a good two feet everywhere she went.

''Sit down, Ella,'' Bryant insisted, cupping her elbow before she reached the stove. ''I'll get this kid's pancakes—this time.'' He eyed the boy reproachfully. ''Not that he couldn't do it himself.''

Shane's cheeks flamed bright red. ''I'm sorry, ma'am. Guess I wasn't thinking.''

''It's all right, Shane. In spite of what my husband might think—'' gratefully, she lowered herself into the chair again ''—I'm not an invalid. Yet.''

Bryant patted her protruding stomach. ''I just don't want you overdoing. You're carrying precious cargo in there.''

The warmth of his caring flooded her senses, and she smiled up at him.

The doctor wanted her to move into Great Falls until the baby arrived, but she was reluctant to leave the ranch—or Bryant. In another week or so she'd have to seriously consider the doctor's recommendation. The weather they'd been having left the roads snow-covered and icy. Given the wintry conditions, the hospital in Great Falls would be a long drive from the Double S. It was hard enough just to get to Reilly's Gulch to handle the bookkeeping chores for Sal and the feed store, and Bryant had insisted he be the one to drive her.

He filled Shane's plate again, drained his own coffee cup and set it on the counter. ''After breakfast, Rusty, I want you and Shane to help me load a couple of sleds with hay. You two can use the big snowmobile to haul the feed up the east side of the home valley. I'll take the smaller one up the west side to catch any stragglers there.''

''You can't go alone,'' Ella objected.

''We won't have that long a break in the weather and one sled can't carry enough for the whole circuit. If those cows don't get some help today, we'll start losing the weaker ones.''

Exasperation had Ella clenching her fists. ''I'm not such a greenhorn that I don't know traveling alone on a day like this can be dangerous. You could fall and hurt yourself and freeze before any help could get to you. I'm going with you.''

"Don't be ridiculous. You're pregnant. You can't risk—"

"I'm not about to let you risk your life, either, by letting you play macho cowboy. You're not going out there alone."

Shane and Rusty studiously kept their eyes on their plates.

"You really think you'd be a lot of help hefting hundred-pound bales of hay off the sled? I don't think so. Not in your condition."

Shoving back her chair, she stood. "My *condition* doesn't prevent me from driving a snowmobile. I'll graciously let you do all the heavy work."

They glared at each other across the table, his eyes narrowed, his brows tugged together. He was really a large man, tall and muscular, easily capable of overpowering her, but she wasn't about to be intimidated. If he could be terminally stubborn, so could she.

"You idolized your mother," she said, seeking a persuasive argument. "What would *she* have done under the same set of circumstances?"

"We usually had more hands."

"But if you didn't?" she persisted.

He didn't answer her, instead tucking his fingertips in his hip pockets. She'd won her point. A *real* rancher's wife wouldn't hesitate a second to do what needed to be done to save the herd.

Under his breath, Rusty said, "I'd let her do it,

boss. Sounds to me like she's a woman who's got her mind made up. And there ain't gonna be no peace 'round here till she gets her way.''

"Thank you, Rusty," she said. Clearing the dishes from the table, she piled them in the sink. "Now, if you gentlemen will excuse me, I'll go upstairs to change into the warmest clothes I can find." Given her "condition," she suspected a thermal tent would be about right.

As she left the room, she heard Bryant swear low and succinctly. She smiled to herself. That man hadn't met a tough rancher's wife until he'd met her. And she was damn well going to prove it today.

BRYANT WENT to get his own cold-weather gear. He wasn't sure what was happening. Ella never backed down from him, and now she was putting herself *and* the baby in harm's way. To save the Double S.

He wanted to believe she cared. About the ranch. About him. But it went against everything life had taught him. Every woman he'd cared about had abandoned him, starting with his own mother. How could he believe Ella would stay? She'd been the one to ask for a temporary marriage—until the baby was born. And the clock was ticking. She'd give birth soon.

Then she'd leave him.

He wrapped a wool scarf around his head and pulled his Stetson down tight.

He wouldn't keep Ella out in the cold long. A

few miles on the snowmobile and they'd be at the line camp. They could warm up there before the return trip home.

He'd keep her safe. And the baby. As long as he was able.

SHE HAD NEVER in her life known true cold until now. In spite of being bundled up in virtually every piece of winter clothing she owned, in spite of a ski mask and goggles, icy fingers sneaked beneath the layers. Granules of snow crept through zippers and frozen air slipped up under her jacket, finding their way to her flesh where they attacked her with a shivering frost. Her lungs burned with each breath.

Grimly she drove the snowmobile along the western edge of the valley, noting pines and firs that used to look sky-high now appeared stunted. The snow was so deep, weakened cows could have collapsed and been buried. It would be spring before the carcasses reappeared.

Riding on the sled behind the snowmobile, Bryant was as exposed to the frigid air as she was. She sensed his tension about the survival of the herd and felt her own.

God's country was an unforgiving place.

Near a sheltered area where trees and boulders formed a natural amphitheater, Bryant ordered her to stop. A forlorn bawling signaled survivors had found a safe haven, but were trapped by the heavy drifts.

Bryant shoveled a path for them through the

snow, then broke open a bale of hay, spreading it across the snow. Hungrily, the cows raced forward to eat their fill, which didn't seem to ease Bryant's grim determination.

"Maybe Rusty and Shane are finding the main herd intact," she said, trying to encourage her husband.

"Maybe." He climbed back onto the sled. "Are you okay?"

"I'm fine." Though feeling warm seemed like a distant memory, and riding on the snowmobile seemed to be compounding the ache in her back.

"The baby?"

Her hand slid across the bulk of her jacket and pants. "He's probably the warmest person in the county."

He nodded. "Let's keep going. If you get too cold, tell me. We'll go back."

No way. She wouldn't give up until Bryant did. And that would only happen when hell did indeed freeze over.

The roar of the snowmobile echoed off the nearby hills, disturbing the pristine scene, a starkly white Christmas card that in reality had the potential to be deadly.

On an exposed slope they found five carcasses, now half buried in snow. Bryant had her drive on.

"Is it warmer on the east side of the valley?" Ella asked.

"A few degrees maybe, with more afternoon sun," he said grimly. "Not enough to make much difference."

The rolling landscape made it impossible to see across the valley, which was several miles wide in places. There was no way to tell if Rusty was finding the main herd had survived or if half the cows had succumbed to the cold.

They stopped at a pond and Bryant hacked a hole in the ice. The sound of the snowmobile drew a few more cows out of the sheltered woods and they eagerly ate the ration of hay Bryant spread on the ground.

Most of the cows' bellies were heavy with their pregnancies. Ella realized that every dead animal they found represented the loss of two head of cattle, not just one, and if the weather didn't moderate soon they'd be losing calves that couldn't manage in the deep snow.

What a dreadfully expensive winter for the Double S.

They'd been gone from the main house for almost an hour. Ella's feet and hands had gone numb; if it weren't for her ski mask, she was sure her nose would be frozen.

That was when a warm gush of liquid spread between her thighs.

Ella killed the throttle and sat back on the seat of the snowmobile. ''Oh, my God,'' she murmured.

''What's wrong? Why did you stop?'' Hopping off the sled, Bryant walked to the snowmobile. There were only a couple of bales of hay left to deliver and then they could stop at the line camp. But not for long. The heavy cloud cover kept dipping lower. In another hour or two they'd be in for more snow.

Her hands still on the handlebars, Ella looked up at him. He couldn't see her eyes behind the dark goggles.

"I think...I think my water broke."

Bryant stood stock-still, letting her words sink into his sluggish brain. "You mean your labor's started?"

"It's too soon. I've got another two weeks before—"

"Babies don't always know how to read a calendar." A feeling of dread filled his gut and fear rose with a bitter taste to his mouth.

Damn, he never should have allowed her to come out here in the cold. But she was such a determined woman, trying to stop her from doing whatever she had on her mind was like standing in front of a train traveling at top speed.

"I'm not in any pain so it can't be labor. But my pants are soaked."

That news jump-started him into action. Being wet in below-freezing temperature was dangerous. And if his memory served him, her labor could start anytime now. Diane's water had broken only minutes before her pains had begun. But they'd been at the hospital with nurses hovering all around.

Not on their own in an isolated valley miles from the ranch house, even farther from suitable medical help.

He hastily disconnected the sled from the snowmobile.

"I'll drive," he told her, mounting the vehicle in front of her.

She scooted out of the way and wrapped her arms around his waist.

"I'm getting you back to the ranch where we can get you warm and figure out what to do next." Doing some quick calculations, he decided they were probably four hours from the hospital—an hour from the ranch house and three on the road.

He flicked the ignition. Nothing happened.

When he got back to the ranch, he'd call the doctor. If necessary—and if the weather held—he'd call for a helicopter to take Ella to the hospital.

He tried to start the vehicle again. Nothing. Only the sound of wind shifting through the treetops.

Damn! Condensation had probably caused water to freeze in the gas tank. All it took was a few drops—

"Bryant!" Her arms tightened around his middle.

"I'm here, honey."

"Labor." He could almost hear her grinding her teeth. "The pains...started."

Beads of sweat formed on his forehead. Desperately he tried to recall what he knew about women giving birth. He'd been through this with Diane. A first-time mother usually spent hours in labor. Just because Ella had felt one labor pain didn't mean she was in crisis yet.

Assuming he could get her to help damn soon.

He gave the ignition another try. Hell, maybe the battery had gone dead. Freezing weather shortened a battery's life by years. Why the hell hadn't he thought to check it?

Mentally inventorying the survival supplies on board, he came up with some energy bars, a tube tent, a few tools and a dinky alcohol stove backpackers carried. No way did he want Ella to give birth with so little protection from the elements.

She groaned softly and the sound ripped through Bryant's gut.

"Another contraction?" he asked.

"I'm afraid so."

"It'll be okay." His remaining options ranked somewhere between poor and dismal.

The first few flakes of snow started to fall as he got off the snowmobile. At the sled, he spread some hay in the center to serve as a thin mattress, then arranged the remaining bales to provide as much protection from the wind and weather as he could. Over it all he stretched out the tube tent like a tarp.

"What are you up to?" Sitting sideways on the useless snowmobile, she was hugging herself against the shivers that had begun to rack her body.

"I'm going to give you a ride on the sled through this winter wonderland." Not wanting to frighten her, Bryant kept his tone light.

"But how? The snowmobile—"

"I'll hitch myself to the sled."

"Bryant, you can't pull me all the way back to the ranch. Can't you signal Rusty? Start a fire or something?"

"We're no more than a half mile to the line cabin. You'll be warm there, and safe."

"You mean I'm going to have the baby at the—" She bent over with another pain.

Striding through the snow, he pulled her into his arms, holding her until the pain eased. "When Rusty gets back to the ranch, he'll realize we've had trouble. He'll come after us. When he finds the snowmobile parked here, he'll know where we've gone for shelter." At least that was what Bryant prayed would happen as he lifted her chin, raised her goggles and looked her straight in the eye. "Try not to worry. We'll still be able to get you to the hospital in plenty of time for Junior's arrival."

"This is my fault, isn't it? I shouldn't have—"

"Shh. It's going to be okay." Palming her cheek, he placed a light kiss on her cold lips. Guilt assailed him. She was going to have his baby and he'd been the one to put her—put them *both*—at risk. He intended to keep them safe or die in the effort.

Circling his arm around her waist, he said, "Let's get you onto the sled and covered up. The sooner we get to the line camp, the sooner we'll both get warm."

He helped her lie down on the sled, then cocooned her with the tarp and a layer of hay to keep her body warmth from escaping.

Harnessing himself with the tow rope, he called to her. "You okay?"

"I'm fine," came her muffled reply.

He took a deep breath with his first step. A half mile. He'd drag Ella and the sled to the end of the world if that was what he had to do to save her and their baby. Dear God, he didn't want to lose her.

Ella peeked out from under the tarp as the sled lurched forward. She was already warmer, the hay providing a small amount of insulation against the cold and the tarp sheltering her from the lightly falling snow.

But Bryant—

Dear heaven! With every step he sank to his knees in the snow, sometimes deeper. How would he ever have the strength to pull her across the uneven, snow-covered terrain for half a mile? He'd need inhuman endurance and stamina.

Her heart constricted with love. That night when she so foolishly climbed into the wrong bed, she certainly found the right cowboy for her. If only he could love her with the same depth of feeling she had for him.

The air cold on her face, she closed the flap on the tarp. Eventually, in the darkness of her makeshift cocoon, she lost track of time, the surging motion of the sled a counterpoint to the contractions that gripped her at increasingly frequent intervals— a counterpoint to the fear that surged within her with each breath she took, with each tightening of her lower body.

She hadn't meant for this to happen. She'd envisioned an easy drive into Great Falls, an unhurried arrival at the hospital. People there to help her. Doctors. Nurses. Bryant holding her hand.

Not this grinding fear that built with each contraction.

She clenched her teeth against a sob. Dear God…

THE SLED had been stopped for several minutes before Ella realized she wasn't moving any longer.

Panic rippled through her. What had happened to Bryant?

Lifting the flap, she discovered it was snowing harder now. Big, fat flakes drifted downward so thickly they obscured the scene. In front of the sled, she could barely make out the shadowed shape of an A-frame cabin with a steeply pitched roof. The line camp!

Scrambling, she made her way out of her hiding place. The icy air chilled her immediately, her wet pants drawing in the cold to start her shivering again. Frantically she looked around for her husband. Then she spotted him sprawled on top of the snow at the end of his ten-foot harness.

"Bryant!" Following in his deep footsteps, staggering, she raced to his side as quickly as she could. Just as she reached him, he regained his feet, breathing heavily, and she knew how much it cost him to move at all.

"Got to get you...inside." Unsteadily, he tried to support her through the snow...and she tried to aid him. Any other man would have totally collapsed by now. But Bryant refused to give up.

Somehow they reached the porch together, both of them shivering. A contraction hit her, grabbing her low and hard. She held on to the doorjamb. Her gloved fingers dug into the wood as she stifled a groan.

God, what a fool she'd been! *City girl.* She would never make it as a rancher's wife.

"Inside," he murmured. "Get a fire going."

It was hard to tell who was helping whom the most or which of them would collapse first. He lit an oil lantern with a wooden match, then got a fire going in the old wood-burning cookstove. With shaking hands, she fed him kindling to build up the flames. The cabin was a single room with a loft. The meager furniture consisted of a table and chairs plus a bed shoved into the far corner.

He dragged the bed closer to the fire, his strength and determination undaunted by the chills that racked him.

"Get out of your clothes," he ordered.

"You, too."

"In a minute."

She stripped off her boots and pants. Still shivering, she slid under the blankets, the sheets as cold as ice.

He took two metal pails outside, filling them with snow and set them on the stove to melt before shedding his own clothes down to his longjohns.

From a cupboard he pulled out two down sleeping bags, piling them on top of the bed, then climbed in beside her. He pulled her into his arms, cradling her. Where his skin touched hers, Bryant felt colder than the snowdrifts outside.

The icy fingers of fear speared through her, rattling her teeth. "What if Rusty doesn't come in time?" she whispered.

"Then we'll make do on our own."

"You can't deliver the baby. You don't know anything about—"

"I've helped a fair number of cows give birth, honey. How different can it be?"

She ought to have a ready answer for that. But before she could think of one, the vise of another contraction closed in on her. She squeezed Bryant's hands so tightly, she expected him to complain. He didn't. He simply gentled his hold around her and rubbed his cheek against her face.

"Remember to breathe, honey."

She tried, but it was hard to concentrate on anything except the pain that racked her body. And this was only the beginning, she knew.

THERE WASN'T MUCH Bryant could do except hold Ella, comforting her as best he could and encouraging her. From time to time, he added fuel to the fire in the old wrought-iron stove and then got back under the covers to cradle her in his arms.

Outside, the gray light of day darkened into night, and the wind kicked up, blowing snow past the window. Bryant knew Rusty wouldn't be able to get to the cabin. Not now. The weather had turned sour. From the looks of things, they were in for a full-scale blizzard. He could take some solace that they'd gotten a load of hay to the herd to stave off their hunger for a while.

But help wouldn't be coming to the cabin anytime soon. They were on their own.

"Bryant! Oh—"

"I'm here. Breathe, sweetheart."

She began panting and he counted—fourteen, fifteen, sixteen. The pains were coming faster now and lasting longer.

Her breathing slowed to normal and she sighed, relaxing against him. "I swear, it must have been a man who said natural birth was the way to go. After ten thousand years of women giving birth, you'd think somebody would come up with a better plan."

He brushed a kiss to her sweat-dampened forehead. "You're tough and you're doing just fine."

"I'm a wimp and I—" Another pain seized her, making her cry out.

"I'm going to take a look," he said, slipping out of bed. The room was noticeably warmer now, the air he breathed no longer fogging in front of his face. Even so, he pulled on his shirt and pants and put on his boots. He'd never known such cold as when he'd been dragging that sled to the cabin.

When her pain stopped, he eased back the covers and had her raise her knees.

"Let's see what's going on," he said.

His stomach knotted when he saw the baby's head was crowning. The cabin was suddenly too hot and he felt drenched in sweat.

His son. Not a calf. Not just anybody's child, someone who meant nothing to Bryant. But his own son.

His chest filled with a frightening combination of love and fear. What if something went wrong? He'd tried so hard to keep an emotional distance from Ella and the baby. And now he couldn't.

Tears blurred his vision. God, he was scared.

"Bryant? What's wrong?"

He swallowed his fears. Ella was counting on him. So was his son. "Nothing. It won't be long now, sweetheart. I can see the baby's head."

She gave him a weak smile. Her hair was damp and mussed, her cheeks pale, her eyes teary behind her glasses. "If you tell me he looks just like the last calf you delivered, I'm gonna kick you."

"He'll be beautiful. Like his mom."

She extended her hand and he took it in his. "I'd rather he looked like you."

He didn't care. Diane's baby hadn't looked at all like him, yet he'd loved Terrilynn and she'd been taken from him. Already he loved this child ten times more.

Until now he'd thought of the baby in general terms. Although Ella had pored over baby-naming books, he'd refused to participate in the exercise. Without a name, the baby didn't exist in Bryant's reality. But seeing the first glimpse of the baby's head, a fifty-cent-size circle of matted hair, his reality had changed.

"What did you decide to name him?" His voice was thick with emotion.

"I thought Jason...Jason Bryant Swain. But if you don't like it—"

"It's a wonderful name. Perfect."

"A good cowboy name."

Bringing her hand to his lips, he kissed her fingers, imagining how he'd teach Jason to ride a horse and cast a line into a good fishing hole. A dozen images came to him, happy pictures of him and his son together, and he wanted to cry out, to plead, "Don't take my son away from me!" But the words stuck in his throat as Ella squeezed down hard on his hand, fighting another contraction.

The pains seemed to go on forever, each one harder and deeper. In between them Bryant got everything ready that he would need—clean linens to wrap the baby in, a knife he'd boiled in water, his own hands scrubbed in hot water until they were red.

"Bryant! Now…I think… Oh, God—"

"Yes, honey, he's coming. Another good push. That's right." He positioned himself between her knees. "Come on, Jason, buddy. Daddy's waiting for you."

With a final scream from Ella and a desperate push, Jason slipped into Bryant's hands. Red. Wrinkled. And in an instant, squalling his objection to the relative chill air of the cabin compared to his mother's womb.

Bryant held the baby, amazement and awe making it difficult for him to take an even breath, the expanding love he felt filling his chest.

Delivering his own son was the most intimate experience he'd ever imagined. The connection was potent, as though he were tied to his son by an invisible umbilical cord so strong that it would never break.

Wrapping the baby in the softest blanket he could find, Bryant lay his son in Ella's arms. "Jason, I'd like you to meet your mother, the strongest, most courageous woman I know."

Chapter Fourteen

Ella's heart squeezed tight as she embraced Jason for the first time. All these months this was the child who'd been growing in her belly. She'd felt him kick his feet and stretch his arms, had imagined this moment. But nothing could compare to actually holding her child in her arms.

Like hundreds of thousands of mothers before her, she loosened the blanket to examine her baby in loving detail. All the right number of fingers and toes. Squinty blue eyes. Almost bald with only a faint cap of ginger-blond hair.

"Definitely you," she whispered, weepy-eyed as she looked up at her husband. "Thank you."

"He's got your eyes." He caressed her cheek with the back of one hand while he stroked Jason's with a single fingertip.

"I hope he doesn't ever need glasses. They're such a pain."

"But cute. On you, at least."

He must be trying to rebuild her ego, she decided. The past however-many hours had done a good job of eliminating any small modicum of modesty she might have retained. Her screams had probably brought down avalanches from mountains miles from the cabin. Majorly wimpy on her part. Still, she smiled at Bryant.

He'd called her courageous.

She didn't feel very brave at the moment. Mostly she felt drained. And so happy, she could barely contain the feeling.

"Whatever you say, *Dr.* Swain."

He grinned back at her. "All things considered, we both did a pretty good job."

"You were wonderful." She sucked in another quick breath as her stomach cramped again.

"Sit tight. We both have a little more work to do."

Within a few minutes Bryant was tenderly bathing her with a warm cloth. His caring and concern amazed her. She knew he loved their son—she could see it in his eyes, could tell by the way he touched the baby. At the same time, she could almost believe he loved her, too, but she was afraid to hope.

When he had her comfortably settled again with the baby snuggled next to her, Bryant asked, "Are you hungry? You want anything?"

"No, I'm fine. I think sleep is what I need."

"You got it. I'm beat, too. I'll stoke the fire, then I'll sleep in the loft." He turned away.

"Bryant?"

"Hmm?"

"After you pump up the fire, could you…could we all sleep together? The three of us?"

He nodded, his throat muscles working, but he didn't speak before he went to take care of the fire.

With heavy eyes, she drifted off to sleep, content when she felt him sliding under the covers next to her again, holding her as he had during the hours of her labor. For the first time she felt as if they were a real family.

SOMETIME LATER, the baby started to fuss.

Bryant lit a lantern so Ella could see what she was doing and she lifted Jason to her breast. With only a little encouragement, the baby found her nipple, tugging gently.

"Lucky kid," Bryant said softly.

"He's lucky to have you for a father."

"I wonder if he'll think so when I have to ground him 'cause he let the stock out of their pen."

"Did you do that?"

He nodded. "I was about nine years old. Dad had a prize heifer he wanted to mate with a bull he'd bought from a guy in Texas."

Absently, he ran his fingertips across the top of Jason's head, an intimate stroking of his son that made Ella's heart clench with a new wave of love.

"For some reason or other, I thought the heifer looked lonely—kind of heartsick—so I let her out of her pen. She trotted off as fast as she could go. I figured she had a boyfriend out on the range and wasn't all that excited about the bull Dad had picked out for her."

Imagining Bryant as a child with romantic notions, Ella had to suppress a giggle. "I gather your father wasn't pleased."

"Not likely. Particularly since that ol' bull got wind of her as she was leaving. He broke out of his pen and hightailed it after her. It took Dad three days to round 'em both up. By then it was too late. There wasn't any way to be sure of the calf's bloodline."

"So you were grounded."

"For a month after that I spent every afternoon when I got home from school mucking out the stalls in the barn and cleaning tack. Fortunately the next year Dad found a couple of heifers who were more cooperative. The offspring of that sturdy old bull have kept our herd going during some pretty rugged winters. Dad was real good when it came to breeding stock."

Taking his hand, she brought it to her lips, kissing him, knowing he was still worried about his cattle. "The herd will make it this year, too."

As though to emphasize his concern, another gust of wind shook the cabin and snow pelted the windows.

"I sure as hell hope so."

The wind was still blowing when she woke again and the delicious smell of baking bread filled the cabin.

Standing by the stove, Bryant announced, "Breakfast is ready. Do you want to eat in bed?"

She glanced at her sleeping baby. "No, I think I'd better move around a little while I can." Gingerly she eased her legs over the side of the bed. She didn't exactly feel like running a race, but all of her aching parts appeared to be in working condition.

Bryant helped her to the table where he had a plate of biscuits and scrambled eggs waiting for her.

"My gracious, if I'd known you could cook, I wouldn't have spent so much time at the ranch slaving over a hot stove fixing meals for you."

"Us macho cowboys are multitalented."

"Now he tells me," she muttered good-naturedly. Discovering she was indeed hungry, she opened a biscuit and watched in delight as steam escaped. "Homemade?"

"From scratch. Unfortunately the eggs are powdered, but they'll do in a pinch. This is what Cliff and I ate when we came up here fishing with Dad."

"You loved your father very much, didn't you?"

"Yeah. I never knew my own father, and I can barely remember my biological mother. Stanley Swain was everything a father ought to be." Sitting down, he thoughtfully studied his plate of eggs. "He loved this ranch. He always told me the land is the only thing a man can count on. I'd cut off my own arm rather than lose it."

Reaching across the table, she covered his hand with hers. "We aren't going to lose the ranch. Not this year or any year. No matter what happens, we're both too stubborn to quit."

He quirked his lips. "When it comes to stubborn, I'd say you're the winner."

"I'll take that as a compliment, Mr. Swain."

"I meant it that way, Mrs. Swain."

Emotion constricted Ella's chest and tightened in her throat. She wished this moment, their time in the cabin together, could go on forever. She'd happily forgo every trace of civilization, she'd live with oil-burning lanterns and a woodstove, if she could always see the love in Bryant's eyes that she saw there now.

Bryant opened his mouth to speak, to ask her what her plans were after they got back to the ranch and if those plans included him, but the distinctive sound of an approaching snowmobile stopped him. Deciding he didn't want to risk knowing the answer just yet, he gave her hand a squeeze and said, "That'll be Rusty coming to our rescue."

"Impeccable timing," she said wryly.

He went to the door and stepped outside. The temperature was only slightly below freezing and the snow had finally stopped after dumping about a foot more on the ground, though the sky still looked a threatening gray.

"Took you long enough to get here," Bryant told his foreman when Rusty switched off the engine. Shane was riding behind the older man on the snowmobile, and they were pulling an empty sled.

"Would of been here sooner 'cept that storm blew in. Couldn't see five feet in front of us by the time we got back to the ranch. Figured you'd be holed up here."

"Is Ella all right?" Shane asked.

Bryant felt a foolish smile stretch his lips. "She's perfect. So's the baby. She gave birth last night."

"Well now, ain't that somethin'," Rusty said. He shoved his hat back farther on his head.

"I helped deliver him."

"That a fact. And it looks to me like you're one proud papa."

Bryant couldn't help himself. His smile grew broader, almost painfully so. Ella had said *we* wouldn't give up the ranch. Maybe she wouldn't leave. Maybe this time a woman Bryant loved wouldn't abandon him.

The word *love* had popped into Bryant's head so easily, he wondered if it had been sitting there on the tip of his mental tongue all along, waiting for him to realize that was exactly what he felt for Ella. A deep, abiding love that could scare a man speechless. Or make him feel like he was walking on clouds.

Somehow he had to find the courage to tell Ella how he felt about her. Tell her before she ended their *temporary* marriage.

"You gonna stand there lookin' like a gooney bird or are you gonna invite us in to meet your son?"

Bryant blinked, focusing again on his foreman.

"His name's Jason…Jason Bryant Swain. And he's gonna be one hell of a cowboy."

WHAT A difference a week could make.

A warm chinook breeze had raised the daytime temperatures above forty degrees, melting the snow, and the roads were plowed and dry all the way to Great Falls. The doctor there had confirmed both

Ella and Jason were doing fine and he dubbed Bryant an excellent emergency obstetrician.

Though winter wasn't over, there was a hint of spring in the air.

Happiness warmed Ella's heart, too, as she prepared dinner, her baby snoozing contentedly in his infant chair nearby. She'd been walking an emotional tightrope since Jason's birth. In every way she could imagine, she and Bryant and the baby seemed like a family. Bryant was always solicitous of her health; he doted on his son, even willing to change diapers or get up in the night to bring the baby to her at feeding time.

Yet however much she felt they were a family, she also felt like a fraud. A pretender.

Her clothes still hung in the guest bedroom. Bryant had spoken of teaching Jason to ride a horse and cast a fishing line, but he'd never said a single word about teaching her.

He hadn't said he loved her.

Swamped by insecurities, she was afraid to be the first to commit herself for fear he wouldn't respond with the love she so desperately wanted. She wouldn't be able to stand the pain if he only suffered her presence because of the baby.

No, if that were the case, she'd have to leave. She wouldn't go far, though. Just back to town. But she knew now she'd never settle for a marriage without love. Her heart simply wouldn't stand the bitter strain of loving without being loved in return.

She switched on the burner under the potatoes she'd peeled and went to the pantry for canned beans she planned to mix with mushroom soup and sprinkle with French onions. Too bad her own kitchen garden had been such a flop. Next year...

The phone rang. Bryant was out in the barn settling the stock for the night, so she hurried to the wall phone in the kitchen, hoping the jarring ring wouldn't wake Jason. Several of the ladies from church had called their congratulations.

"Hello."

A brief pause. "Hi, is, uh, Bryant there?"

"He's out in the barn with the horses. He should be in for dinner soon. Can I take a message for him?"

A longer hesitation. "Uh, who's this?"

She frowned, the man's voice strangely familiar, though she couldn't quite place it. Maybe one of the neighboring ranchers. "This is Ella. Who's calling, please?"

Another pause. "Are you, uh, I mean you sound like... Is this Ella Papadakis?"

"Why, yes, I was...." A shiver of unease crept down her spine. "Who's this?"

"What the heck are you doing at the ranch, Ella? This is Cliff. Cliff Swain."

Her hand tightened around the phone. "I've been here since July." Since her wedding day. "Didn't Bryant mention during any of your phone conversations—"

"Heck no. He never said a word about you. I mean—"

Just then Jason decided he needed some attention and let out a robust cry.

"What's that?" Cliff asked. "It sounded like a baby. Say, what's going on?"

"I think I'd better let your brother tell you."

"No, look, I don't get it. What are you doing at the ranch? Is that *your* baby?"

Despair and disappointment lodged in her throat. "I'll have Bryant call you."

She hung up the phone, then rested her forehead against the cupboard, trying to fight the tears that threatened. She knew for a fact Bryant and Cliff called each other once a month. *Faithfully.* Though Bryant always took Cliff's calls in his office, she'd heard them discussing the herd, news of neighbors and the rustlers that were raiding the herds of local ranchers. When she'd asked Bryant about Cliff, he'd been evasive in his answers, shrugging off her questions as though he didn't want her to realize he'd been talking with his brother.

In all these months, Bryant had never told Cliff he was married. That she was going to have his baby. That she had now produced a son for him, whom he obviously loved.

The phone rang again, but she didn't answer it. She knew Cliff had redialed, curious about her and his brother. She couldn't answer his questions. Not now. Maybe never.

Tears spilled down her cheeks. Her vision blurred, she finally responded to Jason's cries, picking him up and holding him tightly against her chest.

A guest in the house. A pretender. That was all

she'd ever been to Bryant. Not even worthy of mention to his brother.

Her limbs weighted with the pain of rejection, she took the baby upstairs. She'd pack and then she'd leave the ranch. She wouldn't keep Bryant from knowing his son. But she couldn't endure a sham life as Bryant's wife without his love.

Chapter Fifteen

Something was burning.

Bryant smelled it the moment he walked in the back door.

Hurrying to the stove, he grabbed a hot pad and dragged the pot off the burner. From the looks of the contents Ella was planning potatoes à la charcoal for dinner.

There was no sign of her. Jason's vacant infant seat sat in the middle of the kitchen table.

"Ella?" he called, hanging his hat and coat on the peg beside the back door before going in search of her. She probably went upstairs to feed or change the baby and lost track of time. Little Jason could be quite a distraction.

He headed for the nursery, where he found the baby sleeping peacefully in his crib. Reversing course, thinking Ella might have lain down for a nap, he tried the master bedroom but came to an abrupt halt at the door of the guest room instead.

Clothes were scattered across the bed next to an open suitcase. He watched in terrible fascination and growing alarm while Ella grabbed a handful of her underwear from the chest of drawers and stuffed them into the suitcase.

His throat convulsed when he tried to speak and a painful sense of inevitability crowded in his chest, drowning him as though he'd fallen into a bottomless pond. She was leaving. He'd always known she would. But why now? What had happened? He'd hoped for more time.

In some secret place deep inside himself, a place he'd been afraid to acknowledge, he'd hoped for forever.

Finally he forced himself to speak. "What's going on?"

She whirled. Her face was splotchy and red from crying, but her eyes flashed like hot, blue steel. "What am I? Some dirty little secret you thought you had to hide?"

Confusion and panic churned in Bryant's gut. "What are you talking about?"

"Your brother called. Clifford. Remember him? You talk to him once a month, like clockwork. Evidently in all this time, in all the months I've been here—during all the weeks we've been *sleeping* together—my name didn't come up in your conversations. Not even once." She snatched up a couple of blouses from the bed and threw them haphazardly into the suitcase.

"It was a little awkward at first—"

"We've been married for more than six months, Bryant. *Six* months! We've had a baby together.

Don't you think you should have dropped a little hint to your brother?'' On the edge of hysteria, her voice rose to a high pitch. ''A casual mention?''

''A couple of times I tried.'' But he'd been afraid—afraid that if he made too much of Ella being his wife, the mother of his child, that it would hurt all the more when she left. He'd been wrong. Nothing could have hurt more than her leaving now.

''You could have handed me the phone. *I* could have told him.''

''I'm sorry. I'll call him back—explain everything.''

''Explain what?'' Her anger turned to stunned bewilderment. ''My God. Did you think Cliff would be *jealous* of you?''

''No, that's not—''

''Or worse, did you suspect Jason was *his* son, not yours? That I'd lied to you like Diane had?''

He shook his head, and in the face of her determination to leave, he constructed a defensive barrier to protect himself. His heart. His dreams.

''I didn't bother to tell Cliff because I knew damn well you'd be leaving. This whole deal was so your parents wouldn't be ashamed of you getting pregnant without being married, right? Well, I guess you figured you've sacrificed enough. Cliff's call provided a good excuse and now you're ready to move on. Fine by me.''

She'd gone deathly pale and Bryant wanted to go to her, to take Ella in his arms, apologize for what he'd said, but his pride wouldn't let him take the first step. Women he loved abandoned him. That was how it had always been. When push came to shove, Ella would do the same. There wasn't anything he could say or do to change that.

Only this time the woman abandoning him would be taking his son with her. That realization was so painful, it nearly drove him to his knees.

"I never had a chance, did I?" Her whispered accusation sliced through the air like a chill arctic wind. "No matter what I did or how hard I tried, you always expected me to leave. You were counting on it."

"From the beginning you made it clear you wanted our marriage to be temporary. You can't lay the blame for that on me."

"No, I guess I can't." Her gaze, once so full of fury and spark, lost its glitter and slid away from his. She went back to her packing. Methodically she folded each dress, each pair of pants and placed them in the suitcase.

Briefly he considered physically preventing her from taking Jason. But the baby needed her more than he needed Bryant.

A mother could pretty well call the shots, his attorney had once told him. In nine out of ten cases, that was how the courts ruled.

A wail of grief threatened to wrench free of his throat. Bryant barely kept it in check. "When Jason's older...maybe he can visit the ranch. I could still teach him—" During school holidays? Hell, there would never be enough time to do all he wanted to do with his son.

Ella's hands stilled as she was closing the suitcase. "You can see Jason anytime you want to."

Yeah, right. If Bryant was willing to travel to New York or L.A.

"There's no sense for you to rush off. I'll drive you to Great Falls whenever you want. You probably couldn't catch a flight out tonight anyway."

"You don't need to drive me anywhere. I called a cab." She snapped the suitcase closed.

He frowned. A cab? All the way from Great Falls? That would cost a fortune.

Just then he heard a horn honk out front. Damn, how could a taxi get here so fast? He'd wanted more time. Dear God, he wanted a chance to tell his son goodbye.

She lifted the suitcase off the bed.

"I'll carry it," he told her. Their fingers brushed as she let go of the handle, sending sparks of awareness up his arm. It had been weeks since they'd made love; now he'd never have another chance. Never know again the pleasure of holding her in his arms, burying himself in the sweet warmth of her welcoming body.

"I need to pack a bag for Jason and I'll need the infant seat, too. For the cab ride."

"The seat's in the truck. I'll get it." What about the crib? Or did she plan to buy a new one wherever she landed?

"It'll just take me a minute."

"No rush. I'm sure the damn cab will wait." For the fare a guy would charge to take Ella to Great Falls, the cabby would wait half the night.

"I'll send someone for the rest of our things."

"Sure." Like he had a choice.

As he walked downstairs with the suitcase, the festering wounds he'd suffered from repeated abandonments opened again, oozing pain, leaving him with a sense of despair. Somehow his mother had been the first to know. He didn't deserve a family. He wasn't worthy. Somewhere inside he carried a flaw that no amount of time could erase.

He'd tried to burn out that sin by working hard, by loving the land and staying clear of women who could desert him. Nothing had worked.

Then Ella had showed up in his bed—in his life. And the terrible cycle of loss had begun again.

He opened the front door to find Chester O'Reilly standing on his front porch.

"What the hell are you doing here?" Bryant asked.

Chester lifted his brimmed cap, a replica of those worn by New York cab drivers. "I'm CEO and sole driver of Reilly's Gulch's official taxi service. The city council granted me the exclusive contract for the whole darn town. Got me a two-car fleet of cabs."

Bryant was dreaming...except when he pinched himself, he didn't wake up from his nightmare. Ella was still going to leave him. In Chester's taxi? God, nothing made sense.

"Would have brought the Mazda to pick your missus up—she really loves that little car—but I figured a pretty little filly like her would have lots of luggage. So I brought my ol' Buick. Enough trunk space in the old girl to move a cavalry unit." His proud smile shifted his wrinkles like rearranging a three-dimensional terrain map. "They surely don't make 'em like that anymore."

Surely not, but Bryant wasn't interested in discussing the merits of one car over another. He wanted to go back to the way things had been before Ella came into his life—before he'd truly learned how much it could hurt to love a woman and lose her. He'd never experienced this much searing pain before. Not when his mother had abandoned him. Not when Virginia Swain, his adoptive mother, had drawn her final breath in her fight against cancer. And certainly not when Diane had left him.

Together, losing Ella and Jason was a double dose of heartache, enough to drive a man over the edge.

By sheer force of will he held his emotions in check, helping Ella get Jason settled in his car seat. His throat was raw, each unshed tear like a ragged shard of granite, scraping away at his self-control.

Ella got into the car beside the baby. Bryant forced himself to notice every detail he could so he wouldn't forget her—the shape of her glasses resting on her upturned nose, the fullness of her lips, her natural blond hair, the shade of ripening wheat.

"You'll call?" he asked, his voice thick. "Let me know where you and Jason will be?"

She dampened her lips with the tip of her tongue. "I'll call."

He stepped back to close the door.

Chester gunned the old Buick, made a slow circle of the driveway and headed out toward the main road.

Bryant watched until the taillights flickered out of sight. His strength gave way. He sank to his knees in the snow that had melted during the day and was freezing again as the temperature dropped. Only then did he allow himself to cry the bitter, heartbroken tears he hadn't been able to shed as a five-year-old boy.

BRYANT WASN'T SURE how long he stayed like that. But eventually his shivers roused him, a cold that had gone bone deep, and he staggered to his feet.

Beyond consuming a few beers, he wasn't usually a drinking man. In this case a sip or two of medicinal whiskey would be the right thing to do to ward off hypothermia, he rationalized.

He found the dusty bottle on a high shelf in the kitchen. Pulling the stopper, he took a swig. He relished the burning sensation as the liquid slid down his throat and the warmth spread through his gut. He wished Cliff were here. They'd been through a lot together. Loss was easier to handle when there were two of you. Being older by a scant ten minutes, Bryant had always felt he was responsible for his brother. That knowledge helped him keep his emotions in check.

Tonight that little trick Bryant had used for so many years wasn't working. On his own with no need to put on a courageous face, he was an emotional basket case.

Carrying the bottle into the living room, he sat down on the couch in front of the fireplace and stared at the cold ashes. His life was in pretty much the same shape.

He was still in the same position when an insistent knock on the front door woke him—except now he had a whale of a headache and the knocking felt like someone was using a sledgehammer inside his head. Squinting through his bloodshot eyes in the bright light of day, he noted the whiskey bottle lying on the floor at his feet. Empty.

He groaned. God, what a stupid stunt! His mouth tasted like he'd been chewing on loco weed and his tongue was as thick as a cow's.

Walking unsteadily, he made his way to the front door just as the caller pushed it open.

"Well, now, aren't you a sorry sight." Sal stood there glaring at him, her fists on her hips, not an ounce of sympathy in her beady brown eyes.

"Rusty's not here." He turned, planning to leave her standing there, but she grabbed him with her meaty hand.

"Not so fast, cowboy. You can't treat a woman like you've been treating Ella and expect to get away with it."

"What'a ya mean? I didn't do anything. She left *me,* damn it, not the other way around." He shrugged out of her grasp. "Besides, what do you know about Ella anyway?"

"I've been up listening to her weep over your miserable hide half the night, that's what I know."

That statement sobered Bryant. "Where is she?"

"She rented herself and that sweet little baby of yours a room at my hotel, that's where she is. Where'd you expect her to be?"

"Los Angeles?" Or New York. Two thousand miles from Reilly's Gulch by now.

"Not by a long shot, cowboy. Fool woman that she is—and don't you know there's no bigger fool than a woman in love unless it's a man who can't see what's smack in front of his face?—Ella's planning to stay in town. She would have stayed right here on the ranch if you'd had the sense to ask her."

"She would?"

"You've got that damn straight."

"But right upfront she said our marriage was only temporary. I figured—"

"She lied. She wanted a chance to make you love her, though for the life of me, I can't see why." Sal took him by the shoulders, turned him around and headed him up the stairs. "Now we're gonna get you cleaned up, put on your best duds, and you're gonna beg that poor woman to come back here. Not that you deserve her, mind. But that's exactly what you're gonna do—grovel."

She marched him upstairs. If he hadn't dug in his heels, she would have followed him right into the shower and scrubbed him behind the ears. But Bryant didn't need any help. Not now.

Not after Sal had said Ella loved him. That all he needed to do was ask her to stay and she would.

ELLA HADN'T SLEPT a wink, Jason was fussy, and though she'd nursed him several times this morning, nothing seemed to soothe him. Clearly he had picked up on her desperate melancholy and was echoing her turmoil.

Cuddling him on her shoulder, she paced the tiny hotel room over Sal's bar to no avail. He continued to sob, hiccupping between heart-wrenching wails that she couldn't seem to stop. Just as she couldn't seem to halt her own tears.

Her temporary marriage was over. From the beginning Bryant had never given it a chance to succeed. Obviously he didn't want her. He hadn't even bothered to tell Cliff they were married. Or that he'd had a son.

Ella had read him all wrong. She'd been so sure that if he couldn't love her, at least he loved their baby. But he'd let her go, let them both go without so much as a whimper.

The man in the adjacent room pounded on the wall. "Can't you shut that kid up?" he shouted.

"I'm sorry." Sorry about her crying baby; sorry that she'd failed as a wife.

She jiggled Jason up and down, rubbed his back.

The flimsy door to her room burst open, practically coming off its hinges and Bryant raced into the room like a man gone wild.

"What's wrong with Jason? Is he hurt?"

"I don't know. He's just—"

With infinite care, Bryant took the baby from her, cradling Jason to his chest and whispering softly against his cheek. Immediately the wails became snuffling sobs, then quieted altogether as Jason listened intently to his father's soothing voice. Bryant was freshly shaved, his hair slightly damp as though he'd hurriedly left the house after showering. He was wearing a clean shirt, his jeans were nearly new, as though he'd dressed to impress someone.

Ella's heart caught between beats. She wasn't wrong about Bryant loving his son. Maybe there was still hope he could love her, too.

"How did you find us?" she asked when Jason drifted off into contented sleep in Bryant's arms.

"Sal paid me an early-morning call."

"Oh."

"I thought you were leaving for L.A. or points east."

"I told you from the beginning I was going to stay in Montana, in Reilly's Gulch. It's where I want our baby to grow up." Near his father and the man she loved.

He nodded, then said softly, "Sal also pointed out in no uncertain terms that I've been a fool."

A tiny smile threatened. "She does have a way with words, doesn't she?"

Gingerly, Bryant lay Jason on the bed, waiting a moment to see if he'd wake up. The baby slept serenely on, not stirring so much as a stubby-blond eyelash.

Bryant took Ella's hands, his thumb stroking the plain gold band she wore, a symbol of the marriage that he'd only meant to be a temporary one.

"Every woman I've ever loved left me, Ella." The intensity of his blue-eyed gaze flooded her with a jumble of wanting and need. "I know it may seem crazy. Even irrational. But I figured you'd do the same thing. If I let myself love you, you'd leave. As simple—as stupid as that."

He loved her? The baby, yes. That was obvious. The small ray of hope she'd felt earlier grew a little brighter.

"I fought like hell not to let that happen. I tried not to care. I was so damn sure you'd leave if I did."

"I'd never leave you. At least I didn't plan to until I found out you hadn't even told Cliff about me. I was so hurt—"

"It was all part of fooling myself. If I didn't tell my brother, if I didn't let the whole damn world know how much I loved you, then maybe you'd stay."

Breathing became an enormous chore, each intake of air painful. "You wanted me to stay?"

"Oh, yeah, Blondie." Squeezing her hands, he drew her a little closer, until his breath was a sweet whisper of warmth across her face. "I wanted you to stay more than life itself."

"Not just for the baby?"

"I wanted you to stay from the moment you showed up at the ranch looking like a drowned rat. Before I knew you were pregnant. Before I realized how much I loved you."

"Oh, Bryant." She leaned into him, burying her face against his broad chest. The scent of his soap mingled with the lingering base note that was uniquely his own. "I love you so much it hurts. I never wanted to leave you."

"Then stay, Ella. Be my wife, the mother of my child. My children."

She lifted her head. "You want more children?"

"It's a big house. I figure somebody ought to fill all those bedrooms. But before you came along, I didn't believe I deserved a family. If you're willing, I'd like you to fill all those rooms with my babies."

A panicky giggle erupted, one filled with joy. "You're asking an awful lot of a woman who is getting a pretty late start on this motherhood business."

Grinning, he hugged her tight. "It's okay. We Swain boys have a secret weapon. I figure we can double up a time or two with twins. It'll go faster that way."

Feeling light-headed with joy, she said, "Okay, cowboy, give me a few more weeks and we'll get to work breeding some more Swain babies. *One* at a time."

He kissed her gently, his lips both tender and insistent. ''How 'bout we get married again? The right way this time, including a honeymoon. Wherever you want to go, I'll take you there.''

''Perfect,'' she said with a joyful laugh. She'd have her honeymoon at last, a nine-letter word signifying *whoopee!*

*Don't miss the next
irresistible story in Charlotte Maclay's
CAUGHT WITH A COWBOY! duo,
as Tasha Reynolds finds herself
IN A COWBOY'S EMBRACE—
brother-in-law Cliff Swain's!
It's on sale in Harlequin American Romance
in May 2000.*

If you enjoyed what you just read,
then we've got an offer you can't resist!

Take 2 bestselling love stories FREE!

Plus get a FREE surprise gift!

Clip this page and mail it to Harlequin Reader Service®

IN U.S.A.	**IN CANADA**
3010 Walden Ave.	P.O. Box 609
P.O. Box 1867	Fort Erie, Ontario
Buffalo, N.Y. 14240-1867	L2A 5X3

YES! Please send me 2 free Harlequin American Romance® novels and my free surprise gift. Then send me 4 brand-new novels every month, which I will receive months before they're available in stores. In the U.S.A., bill me at the bargain price of $3.57 plus 25¢ delivery per book and applicable sales tax, if any*. In Canada, bill me at the bargain price of $3.96 plus 25¢ delivery per book and applicable taxes**. That's the complete price and a savings of at least 10% off the cover prices—what a great deal! I understand that accepting the 2 free books and gift places me under no obligation ever to buy any books. I can always return a shipment and cancel at any time. Even if I never buy another book from Harlequin, the 2 free books and gift are mine to keep forever. So why not take us up on our invitation. You'll be glad you did!

154 HEN C22W
354 HEN C22X

Name	(PLEASE PRINT)
Address	Apt.#
City	State/Prov. Zip/Postal Code

* Terms and prices subject to change without notice. Sales tax applicable in N.Y.
** Canadian residents will be charged applicable provincial taxes and GST.
  All orders subject to approval. Offer limited to one per household.
  ® are registered trademarks of Harlequin Enterprises Limited.

AMER00   ©1998 Harlequin Enterprises Limited